*W*hat the critics are saying...

&

5 Stars "The suspenseful, romantic mystery of Club de Sade focuses on a woman whose resourcefulness brings her face to face with inexplicable unknowns...The chemistry between Carly Stevens and Jesse Hernandez swelters and electrifies every scene. The exquisite and rich imagery between the characters, as they explore the beginnings of a Dom/sub relationship woven with the intricacies of romance, sent euphoria through this reviewer's system." ~ *Just Erotic Romance Reviews*

4 Angels "...The progress from funny chick lit to sensual and loving D's romance to thrilling suspense makes *Club de Sade* a book to be enjoyed by most readers, it is also good choice for those who want to try the BDSM genre for the first time." ~ *Cupid's Library Reviews*

5 Angels "*Club de Sade* is the story of a nice middle-class girl who gets thrust into the Dominance/submission scene, with hilarious and pleasurable results...Excellently written, with both humorous and serious elements, Club de Sade has something for everyone." ~ *Fallen Angel Review*

"A hilarious and seductive tale of bondage and all it entails, CLUB DE SADE is a fun read. ...Carla's actions are rash, but desperate times call for desperate measures, and her reaction to what actually goes on at BDSM clubs is very funny and realistic. For those of you who enjoy BDSM, or are just a bit curious about what all the fuss is about, take a tour of Claire Thompson's CLUB DE SADE, and find out for yourself." ~ *Romance Reviews Today*

Claire Thompson

Club de Sade

ELLORA'S CAVE
ROMANTICA PUBLISHING

An Ellora's Cave Romantica Publication

www.ellorascave.com

Club De Sade

ISBN#141995346X
ALL RIGHTS RESERVED.
Club De Sade Copyright © 2005 Claire Thompson
Edited by Mary Moran
Cover art by Syneca

Electronic book Publication July 2005
Trade paperback Publication May 2006

Excerpt from *Slave Castle* Copyright © Claire Thompson, 2003

Warning:

The following material contains graphic sexual content meant for mature readers. This story has been rated E–rotic by a minimum of three independent reviewers.

Ellora's Cave Publishing offers three levels of Romantica™ reading entertainment: S (S-ensuous), E (E-rotic), and X (X-treme).

S-ensuous love scenes are explicit and leave nothing to the imagination.

E-rotic love scenes are explicit, leave nothing to the imagination, and are high in volume per the overall word count. In addition, some E-rated titles might contain fantasy material that some readers find objectionable, such as bondage, submission, same sex encounters, forced seductions, and so forth. E-rated titles are the most graphic titles we carry; it is common, for instance, for an author to use words such as "fucking", "cock", "pussy", and such within their work of literature.

X-treme titles differ from E-rated titles only in plot premise and storyline execution. Unlike E-rated titles, stories designated with the letter X tend to contain controversial subject matter not for the faint of heart.

Club de Sade

ॐ

Trademarks Acknowledgement

~

The author acknowledges the trademarked status and trademark owners of the following wordmarks mentioned in this work of fiction:

Brandy Alexander: Ice Cream Bar, Inc.

Barbie: Mattel, Inc.

Macy's: Federated Department Stores, Inc.

Velcro: Velcro Industries B.V. Ltd Liab Co

Chapter One

∽

Carly was so intent on describing her tale of woe that her tuna sandwich sat untouched before her. Eva was nodding sympathetically, her mouth full of fries, her glass of cola poised for a swig.

"Then the bastard actually *thanked* Mr. Downey for the compliment and said he'd been working on the idea for months. The *nerve* of that guy! It was my idea and he knew it. I spent three weeks on that damn proposal and at first he completely ignored it, but as soon as old man Downey took an interest, suddenly it was his idea!"

Carly fumed as Eva calmly took another large bite of her cheeseburger. This wasn't the first time she'd had to listen to Carly rant about her unfair, dominating boss at the clothing catalog company where she worked. This time Eva was prepared, however.

Reaching into her large red handbag she withdrew a classified ad circular and said, "Carly, the time has come for action." As she opened the paper with a flourish she added, "Today we're going to find you a new job!"

Carly lifted her sandwich in both hands but set it down again as she said, "You know I can't just quit. The new fall lineup is coming out and I still have six spreads to do."

"Who cares? You don't owe L.J. Smathers & Co. a damn thing. Franklin's been stealing your ideas since he showed up and dumping all kinds of extra work on you to boot. When's the last time you got a raise?"

Carly fingered the lemon in her water and sighed. "I know. You're right. It's gotten to the point I dread getting up in the morning. I can barely drag myself into work and from the

9

minute I get there, that son of a bitch makes my life a living hell. It's like he gets off on it or something! Sadistic bastard."

"My point exactly," Eva agreed. "Napoleon complex. Little guys who have to lord it over everyone to make up for their short stature and tiny dicks." As Carly grinned her approval at this description, Eva focused on the flyer before her. "I'm not sure we can find anything in publishing or the catalog business, but if you're willing to make a change..."

Eva bent over the circular, red marker in hand. "Let's see. 'Wanted—secretary who can take shorthand and is available on weekends.' Shorthand! Who the hell uses shorthand anymore? And weekends? Forget that." She drew a big red X through the ad. Scanning down the column she continued. "'Wanted—paralegal for New Jersey law firm, competitive salary, references required. Advancement opportunities.' That sounds good."

"Focus, Eva," Carly said, grinning. "We're talking about *me* here, not you!" Eva was a paralegal for a large law firm housed in the same building as Carly's catalog company. She, unlike Carly, liked her job. The two young women had met two years before while eating their sack lunches by the large fountain in the building's courtyard. The friendship had been instant, aided by the loneliness of being a single woman trying to make it in the big city.

Eva continued to scan the columns, circling potential ads and crossing out others. As she turned to the back page she said, "Well, what have we here? My, my, my. I didn't know this was that kind of publication."

"What? What is it? Let me see," Carly craned over the table, trying to read whatever it was that had caught Eva's attention.

Eva, her finger pointing to the spot, read aloud. "'Wanted—Experienced dominatrix. No sex required. Competitive wages plus tips. Hours flexible based on appointments. Call Anthony at Club de Sade, 212-555-8989.'"

Looking around the crowded diner Carly said, "Eva! Lower your voice. We're in a public place."

"So what? It isn't against the law. This looks really cool! I've heard about these places."

"Whorehouses, you mean. Last I heard they were illegal in New York."

"No, no. You heard the ad—no sex required. In fact, any sex at that sort of establishment is against the law. These places cater to freaks and perverts who like to be tied up and spanked while they confess about how they want to suck their mommies' tits. It costs like two hundred dollars an hour for a private session! You would get at least thirty percent, maybe more! You'd probably just have to dress up in black spandex and crack a bullwhip at them while they jerked off."

"You just said no sex." Carly leaned forward, intrigued despite herself by Eva's lurid description.

"Not between you and the, uh, client. No exchange of bodily fluids—that's the deal. But he can jerk off, as long as it's his hand and he comes discreetly into a tissue or something."

"You certainly seem to know a lot about it," Carly remarked, eyeing her friend curiously.

"Well," Eva blushed and ducked her head. "Not really. George took me once, is all." George was Eva's on-again, off-again boyfriend. Right now he was off.

"Once?"

"Well, once or twice."

"And you never told me! I thought we told each other everything."

"Well," Eva answered, recovering her composure. "It was before I knew you. It just never came up in conversation." She pressed her lips together, looking thoroughly embarrassed.

"Okay, I forgive you," Carly laughed. "But anyway, that's nuts. I couldn't do that! I wouldn't know the first thing about it."

"So what's to know? Seems to me all you need to know is it pays well and the hours are flexible. Sounds like a dream job to me. No one stealing your ideas. No one lording it over you and hounding your every move. A bunch of guys kneeling at your feet, desperate to please you or pay the consequences. Can't you just see that bastard Franklin there? Boy, wouldn't that be a switch!"

They giggled together and finished their lunches. As they were walking back to their building Eva said, "So? Are you gonna call or what?"

"Oh, don't be silly, Eva. Even if I did do such a crazy thing, they've probably already filled the position. If it's the piece of cake you say it is, they probably filled it the first day this paper came out."

"Well, miss smarty pants, today *is* the first day. It's Monday, October first. 'The first Monday of each month—all new postings.' See, it says it right there." Eva jabbed her pudgy finger at the front of the circular, which she still carried in her hand.

As they parted at the elevator bank Eva handed the now wrinkled little paper to Carly and said, "Just take it. You'll never know if you don't try."

Back in the office, Carly stuffed the circular into her purse as she sat faced with phone messages to return and budget reports to complete. When had this job shifted from fun to drudge? Actually, she recalled the precise moment—it was when Henry Franklin had been transferred from the Chicago office to the New York office.

Carly who was qualified to fill the position when her former boss left to have a baby and decided not to return, was passed over by management in favor of a man who actually had less direct experience in getting out a catalog, but more time with the company, starting out in their bookkeeping department and working his way up. The fact he was the owner's son-in-law didn't hurt matters for him either.

Chicago's gain was New York's loss, most of the staff quickly agreed, but it was Carly as his personal assistant who took the brunt of his bad temper, his dishonesty with senior management and his domineering attitude.

"Carly! Get in here! Where's that budget for the new men's pants line! I wanted it yesterday!"

"You only gave it to me yesterday," Carly muttered under her breath as she grabbed what she had done so far and stood up.

Murray Shafer, her desk mate, shook his head and whispered, "Don't take it anymore, Carly! Stand up for the masses. Fight!" He shook his fist in the air and grinned.

Mr. Franklin chose that precise moment to stick his head out of his office door, which was right behind their desks. Murray, bold behind the boss's back, now bent his head and began furiously tapping on his computer keyboard.

Suppressing a sigh Carly followed her boss's retreating back into his office.

"Close the door," Franklin snapped. He had resumed his place at his desk, which was set on a slightly raised dais to put his visitors at a height disadvantage. As Carly sat down her boss shifted some papers from one side of his desk to the other for several moments. Carly sat patiently, used to his making her wait.

Eventually he tired of the little game and looked up. "Let's see the numbers, Stevens," he said gruffly, holding out his hand. Carly gave him the one-page rough estimate she had worked up before going to lunch.

"It's not ready, Mr. Franklin," – he insisted on this formality though he called all of his employees by their last names only – Carly answered. "I had to finish approvals for three layouts before I could get to it."

"Always excuses, Stevens. It really gets tedious. I thought you were a gunner. A go-getter. When the boss hands you something and says he wants it tomorrow, you stay up all night if you have to and put it on his desk in the morning before he even gets to work! When I was your age I would have busted my ass for the opportunities you've been afforded."

When you were my age, you were an assistant bookkeeper with no prospects of promotion until you found your way into the boss's daughter's pants! Of course she didn't say this aloud. Franklin liked to perpetuate the myth he had risen by sheer grit and talent. He didn't know the office scuttlebutt had followed him from Chicago via emails with associates there who sent condolences about the new boss.

"You continue to produce half-assed work. You continue to leave on the stroke of five, even when there's work left to be done. You're not a team player, Stevens. You're just out for number one."

Carly sat numbly staring at her hands, wondering what this was really about. She got some idea when he added, his voice now almost a whine. "Why didn't you tell me the new line of children's furniture wasn't ready for production? Why did you throw me to the wolves and make me look like an ass? Do you exist merely to torment me?"

So that was what it was about. The idea he'd stolen, including all her preliminary research for a really clever line of make-it-yourself children's furniture had flopped with management. She'd tried to warn him she still needed to do test marketing before they went forward but as usual he'd ignored her protests.

When top brass had sent out feelers on expanding the clothing line to include other household items, Carly had been excited about the possibilities. But she knew it took time to properly develop and market a new line. Franklin had been in a hurry. He had chided her for being overcautious and taken her idea to the board over her protests. Somehow, her name wasn't even mentioned in connection with the new line. He'd taken her idea and not given her an ounce of credit. It had been as if someone had ripped a baby from her womb. The ache of that injustice had not faded with time. Now, ironically, Franklin had been made to pay the price.

"Mr. Franklin," she said quietly, though she could feel rage like a living thing begin to rise in her blood. "You know I told you that idea wasn't ready." Her smoldering anger gave her a courage she didn't usually possess. "You took something that had a lot of potential and exposed it prematurely. You've killed something that could have been a real boon for this company. You've butchered my idea. I don't know if I can forgive you." Even as she said these words aloud, Carly wanted to take them back. How had she had the nerve — the stupidity — to dare speak such stark truth?

Franklin stood, pressing his palms against the desk as he leaned forward toward her. His face was reddening, his eyes bulging from his head like he was some sort of apoplectic fish. A dribble of spittle appeared on his lip as he hissed, "How *dare* you! I called you in here to explain yourself and you *dare* to accuse *me* of peddling your crummy idea before its time! I've taken a lot of shit from you, Stevens, because I thought you had potential and I wanted to nurture that in you. But this is the last straw! Accusing me of stealing your pathetic little loser furniture line!"

Carly also stood, her hands curled into fists at her sides. Her face was white, her lips pressed tightly together. In a low voice she said, "Mr. Franklin, you are a snake. A vile, repugnant snake who survives by sucking the life out of other people, by stealing their creativity and hard work and claiming it as your own."

"You're fired, Stevens!"

"Wrong, Franklin. You're a second too late. I just quit."

Chapter Two

ഔ

"No way! You called him a vile, repugnant snake?" Eva's voice registered shock and then glee. She giggled through Carly's cell phone.

"I can't believe I did it, Eva. I didn't know I was going to quit when I walked in there. Something just snapped. One injustice too many, I suppose. I just couldn't take one more lie or insult from that son of a bitch."

Carly was standing in the lobby of her building where phone reception was better. When she'd sailed out of Franklin's office, slamming the door behind her, Murray had whistled and said, "Holy shit. What've you done now, Stevens? I could hear raised voices! Not just his, yours, too. You're not gonna be able to sweet-talk yourself out this fine mess, Ollie."

"I just did, Shafer. I quit. I'm outta here. Consider yourself promoted." Grabbing her purse, Carly had fled the office. The first realization she'd just talked herself out of a job was starting to hit home. She had rent to pay in one of the most expensive cities in the world. Her salary had barely covered her fixed expenses and she had no savings to speak of. She had no prospects and now no chance of a decent reference. Tears pricked her eyelids as she punched the down button between the elevators.

Pulling out her cell she had speed-dialed her best friend, not even sure Eva would be able to pick up. Now she said, "I don't know what I've done, Eva. I doubt he'd take me back, even if I got on my knees and begged. I've really blown it this time."

Reliving the scene, she added, "I thought he was going to have a fucking heart attack. You should have seen him." Despite herself, Carly started to giggle. "His face was all red and his eyes were bugging out. It was like a cartoon—I was half expecting steam to come out of his ears. If I hadn't been so damn angry myself, I probably would have laughed in his face."

Sobering she added, "But now he's the one with the last laugh and I'm the one out of a job."

"Oh, sweetie. Listen, I can't leave early, but if you can meet me at The Lemon Café after work, let's sit down and put our heads together. Don't think of this as a door closing. What's that old saying, something about one door closing means another is opening? This could be the best thing that ever happened to you! I'm going to tell you exactly what to do, okay? Now listen to me, are you listening?"

"Yes." Carly felt numb but appreciated her friend was trying to help. She might as well listen. Her own actions obviously got her into trouble.

"Okay, good. Here's what you do. March back up there and collect all your important stuff—the personal stuff you don't want 'disappearing' once they know you're history. And they probably all know it already. Dump it in a box and have somebody there, somebody you trust, keep it for you. Then let Mr. Fuckwad know you're leaving for the day and you'll be back when you're ready to collect whatever you need and have your 'exit interview'. That's what they call it at my job anyway— your 'exit interview'. They probably have something like that there—to ward off lawsuits and make you sign papers and crap absolving them of all liability, etcetera.

"So you just tell Mr. Dickhead you'll be back later in the week to finalize things. You're taking the rest of the day off. Then you go right to Macy's and you buy something nice. Something that will make you feel good. It doesn't have to be expensive, it just has to be something that makes you happy. Then go home and change into something comfy, and meet me at the Lemon at 5:05. 'K?"

"Yes ma'am," Carly intoned. At least she had a plan for the next three hours anyway.

❦ ❦ ❦ ❦ ❦

Eva was sucking her second Brandy Alexander through a straw while Carly sipped some Chardonnay. Carly had just been lamenting about her new unemployed state.

Eva reached for a handful of peanuts and said, "Aren't you forgetting something?"

"What?"

"The want ad! The job for the dominatrix! It was written for you! This is fate, don't you see? Subconsciously you knew it! That's why you were able to quit. Which is something you should have done a long time ago, by the way, and you know that, too. So now you're free to pursue a new and exciting career."

"Oh, come on, Eva. I know nothing about that stuff. I wouldn't know how to dominate some poor guy even if I was willing to. It's not in my nature."

"It doesn't have to be, sweetie. It's an act. You just do it for the money. You are providing a service for which you will be handsomely paid. You just need to prance around in thigh-high black stiletto boots and threaten guys in handcuffs with a spanking. Smack their bare ass a few times. That's all there is to it."

"Since when do you know so much about it? If it's so easy and so wonderful why don't you apply for the job?"

"I told you," Eva said patiently. "I *like* my job. And anyway—" her eyes slid away as she spoke and Carly felt suddenly ashamed. "Look at me. I'm not dominatrix material. They'd take one look at me and say, 'Next!'"

Eva was overweight. This wasn't something they discussed and Eva usually seemed at peace with it. She certainly didn't diet, subsisting on cheeseburgers, fries and milkshakes almost daily, not to mention her favorite alcoholic beverage—a Brandy Alexander made with extra creamy vanilla ice cream. Her boyfriend George was overweight, too, and it didn't seem to stop them from having a very satisfying sex life—that is when they hadn't just broken up over something stupid.

Carly on the other hand was petite but lithe. Though small, she was strong with lean muscles and curves that made men's hearts ache. Eva liked to call her the girl from Ipanema, after the famous Portuguese jazz song.

"No way," Carla would laugh. "I'm too short. The girl from Ipanema was tall, tall, tall." Carly was only five-foot-two.

"Six-inch heels will fix that! Come on, girl. I can totally see you in black leather, wielding a whip while the boys scamper around you like puppies on their hands and knees."

"Eva!" Carly laughed, partly shocked but also partly intrigued. The wine was doing its work, lowering some of her defenses. The shock of the whole day must have been getting to her because she suddenly felt overwhelmed with fatigue.

"So, you'll do it? Come on, Carly. Say yes. Say you'll at least call and find out more about it tomorrow. Promise?"

"All right, all right. I promise. Tomorrow."

* * * * *

Carly slept late the next morning, something she rarely did even on weekends. She awoke groggy and out of sorts. They'd stayed at The Lemon Café until after midnight drinking more than was good for either of them. Poor Eva would be exhausted, Carly thought sympathetically, knowing Eva had to be at work by eight-thirty. She herself had to report at eight o'clock. How odd to have slept right up until ten o'clock. Usually Carly was awake a few minutes before her six o'clock alarm, letting herself come fully conscious before the radio clicked on, at which time she would get right out of bed to start the day.

Not today. Today she lay in bed for another twenty minutes after she awoke. Her mind roamed over the events of the day before. She marveled anew that she'd dared to have it out at last with that bastard Franklin. Today however, along with the incredulity and downright fear at her new situation, Carly experienced another sensation—pride. Pride at her courage. She'd dared to stand up to the biggest bully she'd ever known. And she hadn't died. She hadn't even cried! She'd just walked right out of there—her head held high, her coworkers staring in awe.

Now she was unemployed, it was true. But hey, she hadn't had a job when she found that one. She could definitely find something in this town. And if not in this town, why she'd go somewhere else! It was a big world out there. She smiled and sat up.

The phone rang and she reached to answer it. "Hello?"

"Hiya. Didja do it?" Eva sounded breathless. It was break time at her law office.

"Do what?"

"Call, silly! Did you call Club de Sade?"

"Jesus, Eva, give it a rest! I just woke up."

"Just woke up! Man, it must be nice, the life of the leisure class." Carly stood and stretched, taking a deep breath and blowing it out. Eva continued, "But seriously, Carly. You promised."

"All right. All *right*! You just aren't going to shut up about this until I call, are you?"

"Nope."

"Okay, okay. I'll call. I'm sure the position is filled by now, but anything to make you happy, Mistress."

Eva laughed. "Now you're talking! See, you're already into the spirit of the thing. Mistress—" she laughed again "—that was a good one." The phone clicked and she was gone.

Carly poured coffee and sat down at her tiny kitchen table in the little kitchenette with barely room for one person to turn around in. She had brought her phone over as well as the classified ads circular, folded so the ad in question was showing, circled in red by Eva.

She read it again, wondering what it would be like to have such a job. Was it any different than being a prostitute? Prostitutes sold their bodies for money. That was illegal. Not that Carly believed there was any moral failing in selling your sexual favors. If someone wanted to pay and you wanted to sell, whose business was it? But she knew the reality was it was illegal, dangerous and sometimes even fatal for the women who were involved in it.

This seemed different though. This was more like selling fantasy. Selling a dream. A strange dream, she had to admit. A tiny part of her understood. Though it was completely unexplored in real life, she had had her own occasional fantasy of being "taken by force". She supposed it was every woman's fantasy to some degree — the primal idea of a strong man taking possession of you. Claiming you like the caveman knocking his woman on the head and dragging her to a cave to "have his way" with her. Maybe that was all it was — a deeply ingrained ancient response to seek out the dominant male so he would perpetuate the species by creating offspring.

How technical, how clinical, she thought and shrugged. This wasn't about that, at least not directly. And it wasn't women who were asking to buy this particular fantasy. She paused with her coffee cup midway to her lips. Was it? The ad really didn't specify exactly who used these services. Would she be expected to spank *women*, too?

The whole thing was too weird. Well, all she'd promised Eva was a phone call. She could handle that much. What the hell? It was anonymous anyway at this point. She clicked the phone on and punched in the numbers. After a second it connected and after three rings someone answered, "Club de Sade. Anthony at your service."

"Oh, uh," Carly hesitated and then plunged on. "I was calling about the dominatrix ad? The, uh, position at the club?"

"Yes, what did you want to know?"

His voice was low and smooth with a Latin hint. He hadn't said it was filled and so she continued, "Uh, well, is it still available? Are you scheduling interviews?"

"Yes, it's still available." He paused a moment and Carly could hear paper rustling in the background. "Let's see. I have to leave in a bit. Let's see, could you be here at eleven o'clock? I know it's early but this is when I have time..."

Carly glanced at the wall clock. It was already ten-thirty. The address wasn't far from her apartment though and if she caught a bus she should be able to be there in time. No time to shower, though! And what would she wear?

Not one to look a gift horse in the mouth however, she said simply, "I think I can make it. My name's Carly Stevens."

"And you have experience, yes?"

"Tons."

"Great. See you in thirty."

* * * * *

"You did say you're a pro, right? Experienced? Don't you have your own wardrobe?" The interview had been going well up to that point, she thought. They seemed to have a nice rapport from the get-go. Anthony was obviously gay, even effeminate, but this didn't bother Carly. Her best friend in college had been gay and Anthony reminded her of him. This alone made her relax and things had gone well until she'd goofed and asked what she was supposed to wear on the job.

She'd tried to hem and haw her way out of it by claiming some clubs she'd worked for had their own uniforms and she just needed to know what Club de Sade's policy was.

"Oh, anything at all, as long as it's black and as long as it's leather," Anthony laughed. "If you need some new stuff, Leather and Lace over in the Village is the place to go."

Anthony laid out the terms of employment—Eva was right about the house charge—two hundred dollars per hour, but had underestimated Carly's take if she landed the job. "You get one hundred dollars an hour after the first two-week period, where you'll only get fifty because you'll be on probation. But if you 'pass the audition' as they say — that is, if the clients like you and you start to develop a following, you get a hundred, plus tips. We have a healthcare plan, too, once you'd been here six months and two weeks paid vacation after one year."

"Just like a real job," Carly laughed and then put her hand to mouth, certain she'd insulted him. But Anthony laughed along with her.

"Honey, I like you," he said. "You don't take yourself too seriously. Some Doms, they just think they hung the moon. You must always address them as 'sir' or 'ma'am' and they're always in character. It can get old really fast, believe you me."

Carly glanced at her watch. They'd been talking for about thirty minutes. Anthony had explained the rules of the club. Again Eva had been right — no "exchange of bodily fluids" permitted — but just about everything else went. Nudity was okay. Whipping, paddling, cuffs, bondage and hot wax were all fine. And yes, the clients were permitted to ejaculate, as long as it didn't touch the staff.

"I like to make them lick it up," Anthony said, an evil gleam in his eye. "Oh, and no blood. That's another no-no. Can't draw blood."

"Who would want to do that?" Carly was scandalized and forgot to hide it.

"Honey, people will do anything to get their rocks off. Surely you know that. We've got a couple of regulars who favor knife play. They like to jerk off while someone holds a blade to their throat and threatens to slit it. Sick stuff maybe, but hey, who's to judge what turns people on? As long as it doesn't hurt anyone else, what's the big deal? Safe, sane and consensual — those are our bywords."

"How many hours a week would I be expected to work?"

"Minimum of twenty — at first you'll mainly cover the walk-ins as you start to build up your own clientele. Do you have your own regulars you'll be bringing?" As Carly shook her head he continued. "Well, I can promise you twenty. However much over that is up to you.

"Other than house parties, which we hold about once a month, you can make your own hours. One's coming up, in fact. Sometimes I'll ask you to cover for someone if they're sick or whatever. I'm here by ten o'clock most mornings. We get a lot of day appointments, as I'm sure you're used to. Judges on their way to the courthouse needing a good spanking or a surgeon who likes to be tied up between rounds at the hospital. Most of them are married, with wives who would rather die than tie them up and give them what they need.

"Which reminds me — I'm sure you know this, but just to make sure it's clear — strict confidentiality is crucial. You don't tell your husband, your mom, your lover, anybody, the names of our clients. We'd be out of business in a New York minute if these guys didn't trust in our ability to keep their, uh, activities, discreet. That goes without saying, but I figured I'd better say it anyway."

Carly nodded. What he was saying made sense though she hadn't thought about it until he'd mentioned it. He continued. "You can work sixty hours a week if you have the energy. But as you know, it's an *exhausting* business. Being a Dom is a lot of work!" He grinned conspiratorially and Carly tried to look world-weary and knowledgeable about the whole thing.

"We're open six days a week — closed Mondays. Even perverts need time off!" He laughed musically, the tones tripping down a major scale. "You'll get your own key once you've been here two weeks. Meanwhile you can use the office key during working hours. I keep it on a peg on the side of my desk. If you have to schedule something before ten in the morning, let me know. I'll make sure to be here. Amanda has a policy — no women here alone with a client. Usually they're harmless but you never know. The occasional passive pussycat can become a tiger if you push the wrong buttons."

As Carly looked alarmed Anthony patted her hand and said, "Don't worry, honey. If you get the job, big, strong Anthony will be here to protect you." He flexed his biceps in his silk T-shirt. They really were quite developed, courtesy of his local gym, no doubt. He laughed and added, "I'm here all the time. I practically *live* here. If Amanda doesn't get me some clerical and phone help soon, I swear to all the saints I'm going to lose my *mind*! I barely have time for my own clients now, what with running this whole show by myself!" He sounded both affronted and proud.

"Now, about references…" Anthony looked at her, his expression expectant.

It was the moment she had been dreading and now it was here. Carly felt her mind go blank. *Think*, she admonished herself. Stammering a little she said, "Uh, actually, I didn't bring any names or anything. My clientele here is primarily private. You know the business. It's so, uh, confidential." She seized on his earlier comments on the importance of confidentiality.

When he didn't respond immediately she hurried on. "That is, uh, I could probably get you a reference from a club I worked in in California a while back, but honestly I'm not sure it's even open anymore…" Carly trailed off, her face hot, her gut twisting. She hated lying.

She stared down, her fingers twisting nervously in her lap, waiting for Anthony to stand up, extend his hand and say he'd be getting back to her. Instead she heard him say, "Hey, don't worry about it." Leaning forward confidentially he said, "Listen, between you and me, I don't usually even check references. I mean, you can always find someone to say something positive about you. This kind of job isn't like a corporation where some impersonal bureaucrat fills out forms on your performance. It's a subjective thing."

Carly dared to look up, tendrils of hope suddenly shooting up through her disappointment. He went on, "I like you, Carly. I like what I see. Why don't I show you around a little and we can talk some more afterwards."

He took her on a tour of the facilities. The club was actually a converted three-story brownstone with a finished basement. The main floor contained a front hall, parlor, kitchen and library. One side of the library had been converted to an office and this was where Anthony had conducted Carly's interview. It was a large room, with several couches and chairs set about. Anthony had told her this was where the staff came to "cool off" between clients.

The parlor was set up like a waiting area, with more comfortable couches and chairs. A television had been mounted on brackets on the wall and though that morning the screen was dark Anthony said, "Usually we have some S&M flick running, to get them in the mood if they aren't already." He winked at her.

The kitchen, an old, dark affair complete with a butler's pantry, wasn't used much, Anthony explained, except for the refrigerator that some of the staff used to keep their lunches and dinners if they didn't order takeout. "I have a little fridge in my office where we keep some soft drinks, though. We mostly use that.

"Come on, I'll show you upstairs. Oh, not those," he said as Carly moved to the narrow steep stairs just off the kitchen. "No one uses those. They're too steep. That was the old servants passage, I guess. Come on."

He led her back to the front hallway, which ended at the broad curving stairway. As they climbed the old oak stairs Anthony said, "Up here is where we take our private clients. One-on-one stuff." Carly nodded vaguely, wondering what she was doing here. He led her down a narrow hall and opened one of the doors. "They're all pretty much like this. We have ten rooms available but they're rarely all in use, except on party nights."

The room looked much like any hotel guestroom, with a large double bed and a little bureau. The one chair in the room was a tall formidable-looking thing with leather cuffs on the arms and legs and a thick leather belt resting empty on the seat. The chair legs appeared to be adjustable with a small crank on the side of the chair so the occupant's legs could be spread.

As Carly stared at the chair Anthony grinned. "Cool, huh? Amanda's S.O., her significant other, designed it for us. Our very own 'torture chairs'. We have one in every room."

"And you, uh, use it? I mean, you put people in these chairs?"

"Sure, why not? If they want it, that is. This is all voluntary, obviously. People pay good money so sexy women like you will tie them down, whip their sorry asses and maybe let them jerk off while you call them names. It's no big deal. I mean, you know that, right? You *did* say you had experience, didn't you?" He eyed her sharply.

"Yes, yes, I did, yes," Carly hurriedly responded.

Seemingly satisfied, Anthony pointed to a large plastic timer on the little night table next to the bed. There was also a telephone next to it. "We do one-hour sessions, so don't forget to start the timer when they enter the room. That way there's no arguing about how much time has passed. They know once the timer dings, they're done. Unless of course they want to cough up more money for a longer session. That phone doesn't have an outside line, but you can call downstairs with it if you need anything or there's an emergency."

"Emergency?"

"The client gets out of control or they start trying to mess with you sexually. The usual."

"Ah," Carly said faintly. What was she doing here?

Anthony blithely continued. "Next floor is same as this one. The rooms are smaller, though. We don't usually have enough clients at any one time to use that floor though. Sometimes you can go up there and catch a nap if you want."

He took her downstairs again, this time all the way to the basement. The room was dimly lit and the black painted walls didn't add any light to the décor. The room was lined with straight-backed wooden chairs. Placed about the room were several of those "torture chairs" as well as two gynecological tables complete with stirrups and a whole array of whips, crops and floggers hung here and there on the walls. Along one wall a raised stage had been built. Above it, two thick metal bars hung parallel to the ceiling, suspended by chains.

"Welcome to the Dungeon de Sade," Anthony had said in a theatrical tone, his arm sweeping out in a grand gesture. "This is where it really happens. Our big events. You'll be expected to attend the parties and to serve as a resident Mistress. Your duties will be the usual—demonstrate whipping techniques to the novices, let some poor slob lick your boots, run a slave auction or two.

"Some heavy scene play goes on here, especially when we host seminars or Roses and Thorns parties."

Whatever those are, Carly thought.

As she dubiously eyed the bars hanging over the little stage Anthony offered in a matter-of-fact tone, "Those come in handy for displays and public whippings." Carly nodded with what she hoped was a nonchalant air. He led her over to the side of the room where a tall, thick post had been cemented into the floor. It stood about seven feet high and about twelve inches in diameter, the wood rubbed smooth from years of use. An iron wrist cuff was bolted to either side of the post.

As he ran his hand sensually up the smooth wood Anthony said reverently, "And this is a whipping post. It's a real one. Amanda, the owner, found it over in Asia somewhere. It's so deliciously *phallic*, don't you think? They still use these things in some countries for public punishment. But here it's just for fun, of course."

"Of course," Carly echoed faintly.

They were silent as Anthony led her back to his office in the library. Carly's mind was churning. Could she do this stuff? How hard could it be? He'd assured her no sex was involved.

She'd have to get herself trained in all this whipping technique stuff, but again, how hard could it be?

When they sat again in his office Anthony crossed his long legs and leaned toward her. "So, any questions? What do you think of our little establishment? *Tres chic, n'est pas*?" His tone bespoke his own clear pride in the operation.

"Quite impressive," Carly responded sincerely. She didn't add she'd never seen anything like it in her life! She knew she should have some intelligent questions to put forth, but frankly, she felt so overwhelmed by the whole thing her mind was a blank. Somehow, she'd skirted the whole reference issue and now the moment was at hand. Casually she asked, "So when do you think I'll hear from you?"

"Right now."

"Excuse me?"

"I mean, if you want the job, you're hired. When can you start?" As Carly stared dumbfounded Anthony added, "Are you surprised? A gorgeous woman like you? I may be gay but I have eyes in my head!"

As he sat behind his desk Anthony continued. "Between you and me, sweetheart, you had the job before you opened your mouth. The three I interviewed yesterday were all washouts. You have to have a certain *something* to pull this off, as you obviously know, being experienced and all. Not everyone can do it. But I can tell — you have a certain flair." He patted her hand and said, "Honey, all you had to do was speak English and know how to hold a whip and baby, this job was yours."

Carly swallowed and smiled weakly. She appreciated the compliments regarding her person but knew she'd just gotten a job under false pretenses. She *didn't* know how to hold a whip! She didn't even own a whip!

Yet she found herself extending her hand and smiling. "Thank you, Anthony. I really appreciate this opportunity. I can start one week from today."

"Lady, you've got yourself a deal."

✦ ✦ ✦ ✦ ✦

Carly stood in front of a row of black leather outfits. Some of them cost two and three hundred dollars, just for the bustier! Anthony had told her this place, Leather and Lace Boutique was the best place to get the outfits he expected her to wear on the job. She was also expected to purchase her own.

As she rifled through outfits, looking for something proper for a Dominatrix such as herself, a thin young woman approached her. She was dressed in a bright red corset that pushed her rather small breasts up and together. The bodice was cut so low Carly could see the top halves of her little brown nipples. She looked away, embarrassed. Yet the girl seemed perfectly at ease. The corset sat atop blue jeans, a rather odd combination.

Her little pixie face was heavily made-up, with thick eyeliner ringing her eyes. Carly doubted she could be much over eighteen. The girl smiled and said, "Can I help you, ma'am? Would you like to try some of these on? You really can't tell with leather unless you try it on."

The girl eyed Carly critically and offered, "You're kind of short. Breasts are good though—not too big, not too small." She paused, tilting her head appraisingly. "There isn't going to be much selection for your size but I do have some things that might work. Come over here to this petite rack."

Carly wasn't offended by the girl's frank assessment, as she could see she was honestly trying to help her. Obediently she followed the saleswoman to a rack containing more bustiers and leather pants. Carly selected several items to try and draped them over her arm.

"You'll need boots, too. Or heels. We have some great stuff on sale right now. Let me show you." Carly spent the next hour trying on clothing that was difficult to get on but, she had to admit, looked pretty hot once she was in it. Her short, tussled honey blonde hair was set off rather nicely by the black soft leathers she chose. Her round, high breasts looked alluring in the little vest, the zipper pulled lower than she would ever dare "in real life". This didn't seem real yet.

She still had a week to figure out what the hell she was doing. The idea of an entire week off seemed like its own piece of heaven to Carly who had worked since she was seventeen years old.

The salesgirl who told Carly her name was Audrey, was really quite helpful. She showed Carly what to look for in terms of quality and cut. "You were born to wear this stuff. You have the perfect figure for leather. I mean, you're short but you have a great shape. Your tits look really hot in that vest."

Carly had blushed at the girl's outspoken remarks but Audrey had said them without guile or intent to shock. It was a whole different world, Carly was beginning to suspect. A secret subculture — this "scene" — where normal mores of behavior simply didn't apply. She would have to feel her way as she went.

Audrey rang up her purchases to the tune of five hundred and fifty-three dollars Carly definitely didn't have to spend at this point. As she watched Audrey drape plastic over the hangers Carly had a sudden inspiration. "Say, Audrey. I have a question. Do you know where I could take, uh, lessons in 'the scene'? You know, like 'How to be a Dominatrix'? That kind of thing?"

Audrey had stared at her a second and then laughed. "You're putting me on, right? Kidding around? You want lessons in how to whip a guy, is that it?"

"Well, kind of, yes." Carly felt ridiculous.

"Well, I don't know." Audrey squinted at the ceiling a moment. "Wait, I do have something here actually. Here in the window. Look. It's a kind of calendar thing. We let people post stuff about events and things for sale. See? Sometimes there are seminars and classes. You could check it out."

"Thanks. Thanks for all your help, Audrey."

"It's cool. I get commissions. You've made my day!" Audrey grinned and this made her look like the kid she was.

Carly, only twenty-six herself, suddenly felt old and wise by comparison. She stepped over to the window and started to read the posters and flyers there. She scanned the ads, her eyebrows rising as she read things like *Wanted – Cruel Mistress for 24/7 Degradation*, and *Required – She-male with Foot Fetish. Must be willing to do housework.*

She read several ads seeking used "scene" equipment and selling the same. Things like *Original Adam's Blue Suede Flogger – $150 – must sell.* That was the used price? Several other ads included items for sale or purchase and the prices only went up from there. Apparently this was an expensive business! Was she supposed to bring her own "toys"? She realized a call to Anthony was in order. What was she getting herself into?

There were in fact several seminars being offered and Carly homed in on these. *Bullwhips, Floggers and Crops – A Lesson in Obedience Training.* It was scheduled for the coming week at a little club with an address she didn't recognize. It sounded a little too intense for her purposes. Obedience training? Again she found herself wondering what she was getting herself into. She read a few more flyers until she came across *Dominance 101 – What You Need to Know for Responsible Ownership.*

She had to grin a little. Ownership, huh? These groups seemed to take themselves rather seriously. Well, it did seem to fit the bill at least in terms of the "101" part. She certainly knew nothing about it. She read the fine print, noticed it was being offered by the Roses and Thorns Society and it was being held on Wednesday, October third at eight o'clock in the evening at the Paddler Club in SoHo. *Members only or by special reservation. Call Jake at 212-555-3003 for reservations and price information.*

Carly thought a moment – Wednesday, that was tomorrow! This was all happening so fast. She'd have to call this Jake person right away if she was going to learn something. Should she do it or just "wing it" as a Dominatrix come next Monday?

Carly was an organized person, the kind of girl who had always had her term paper done well in advance of the due date. She was not a "by-the-seat-of-your-pants" kind of a woman. She liked to know what was expected and be prepared. She knew she would be calling Jake, but at least she'd wait until she made it home with her new Dominatrix wardrobe.

Once in her apartment Carly sat down at her little kitchen table and studied the scrap of paper on which she'd scrawled the phone number. In what had become almost a mantra she muttered, "What am I getting myself into?" as she punched in the numbers.

"Hi, you've reached Jake Mitchell. I can't come to the phone right now, but please leave your name and number and I'll get back to you as soon as possible. Yours in bondage." His voice was deep and rumbly, but he sounded friendly.

Yours in bondage? Please. Feeling a little silly, Carly left her name and number and the fact she was interested in the seminar being offered on Wednesday. She hoped there was still an opening. She'd lied to get this job and now if she showed up like some novice jackass she'd probably be fired by the end of the day. What had been in her head when she went for that interview? This was so unlike her—doing anything at the drop of a hat went against her grain.

It must have been some kind of rebound from quitting her job. She'd never done anything like that before either. Though that job had been a dead end for some time. Instead of cursing out that bastard Franklin, maybe she should be thanking him. Now instead of dragging herself to a nine-to-fiver—well, more like an eight-to-sixer!—she was going to set her own hours, get paid more than twice what she had been making—with health benefits. This made her grin—it seemed incongruous somehow for perverts to offer health insurance—and her whole job was to make some poor guy bend over and get spanked.

What a strange twist her life was taking. She jumped when the phone rang. She could see on the caller ID it was Jake

Mitchell and quickly she grabbed the receiver and clicked it on. "Hello?"

"Hi, is this Carly?"

"Yes, this is Carly Stevens."

"Hi, Jake Mitchell here. You called about the seminar?"

"Yes, I was wondering if you still had openings? And how much is it? And could you tell me a little about it?"

"Okay, sure. Yes, there are still openings. It's held at the Paddler Club and they have space for like fifty people in their main room. We only have thirty-eight signed up. The cost is seventy-five dollars for a two-hour seminar. We supply the whips for training purposes but feel free to bring your own favorite toys. Plenty of slaves will be on hand for demonstration purposes." He rattled on with details about the training and finally asked, "So, shall I put your name down?"

"Yes," Carly said before she had a chance to change her mind. "I'll be there. Eight o'clock tomorrow."

"Great. See you then."

Chapter Three

ဆဂ

The Paddler Club wasn't nearly as nice as Club de Sade, Carly decided. It was a tiny space, just a basement room underneath a fetish clothing shop. She wouldn't have known it was there except for Jake's explicit directions. As she walked down the crumbling concrete stairs, she thought about Eva's offer earlier in the day to come with her.

Carly had declined, certain Eva would make her feel even more self-conscious than she already felt. The last thing she needed was Eva's running commentary about any and everything.

Predictably, Eva had ooh'ed and aah'ed over Carly's vivid description of her job interview. "He said you were gorgeous and sexy? How cool is that! I've always *told* you that, haven't I? Why you don't have boyfriends galore is beyond me!"

Carly changed the subject, one which always made her uncomfortable. Men were usually attracted to her but she rarely responded. Most men bored her, she found. She secretly wondered if there wasn't something wrong with her — if she was incapable of the intensity of feeling necessary to fall in love. She didn't like to dwell on this, however, or the fact that at twenty-six she was still single and had yet to sustain a committed relationship.

She told Eva about the money and the benefits, and they chuckled a little bit about how mundane it all sounded. Eva asked, "So, you're really going to do it? You took the job?"

"I really did. I can't believe it myself. I'll probably get fired after the first day. I have no clue what I'm doing. But I'm going to a seminar tomorrow. A 'how-to' kind of thing, at least I hope it is."

And now here she was, handing her money to a round, balding man with a good-natured face who was scanning his legal pad for her name. "Ah yes, here it is. Carly Stevens. You called yesterday, right?"

She recognized his voice. "You're Jake?"

"One and the same," he said, holding out a very hairy arm by way of greeting. Carly shook his hand and smiled nervously.

"You a newbie?"

"Excuse me?"

"Newbie. New to the scene."

"Um, yes, I guess you could say that." Carly felt embarrassed but what was the point of lying? This guy wasn't offering her a job.

Jake grinned at her and said, "Well, you've come to the right place. This is my favorite seminar because we really get down to basics. No esoteric bullshit about subspace and how to use a violet wand or any of that shit. Just plain basic how to pick a whip, how to use a whip, how to show your sub the ropes. You Dom or sub?"

The question was unexpected as she was still trying to process what he was talking about. Subspace? Violet wand? What was he saying? Apparently there was a whole lingo she had better learn and pronto. She made a mental note to get online as soon as she got home and read up on her new "profession".

Meanwhile she said, "Dom. Dominatrix. Professional Dominatrix." She grinned, suddenly enjoying her newly adopted status. She was a Domme, wasn't she? After all, someone was willing to pay her big bucks to hold that title.

Jake eyed her, his expression dubious. "Dom, huh? I had you pegged for sub, quite frankly. Sent here by your master to learn the ropes for reasons of his own. You've got that certain something…" When Carly didn't respond he added, "Well, just shows you can't always tell." He looked at her more closely, leaning across the little bar that separated them so his face was uncomfortably close and she felt compelled to step back.

"I don't know," he mused, "I'd say you're sub. I'm rarely wrong."

Carly bridled and stood straighter. She was wearing her new black leather boots and leather pants, though she'd chickened out at the last moment and opted for a white silk blouse instead of the revealing black leather vest that completed the ensemble. "Well, guess there's always a first time," she said haughtily.

Jake sat back, smiling blandly and said, "Yeah, whatever. Well, go on in there. We only have one speaker tonight, but he's one of the best. Just find a seat where you like. There's juice and soda at the bar there. No smoking."

He pointed into the dark little room and Carly entered. The walls were painted a garish red with televisions placed on little mounted stands near the ceiling all around the room. Porn videos were playing with the sound turned off—a different video on each set. Carly felt herself blushing and mentally chided herself. She'd better get used to it!

She looked around the room. There were quite a few people milling around. They all seemed to know one another—standing in little clusters chatting, drinks in hand. Most of the people were in "fetish" wear—black leather and shiny latex, with some of the outfits leaving very little to the imagination.

Most of the people were men, she noticed. Of the dozen or so women there, she did observe a number of them were rather chubby, even fat, but this didn't stop them from dressing in skin-tight leathers and skirts, their heavy bosoms heaving over tight corsets and bustiers. Not all of the women were heavy, however. Carly especially noticed a striking woman of about forty, her auburn hair flowing down her back, her long legs bare beneath a tight red leather miniskirt. Carly noticed the woman had a chain around her neck like a collar with a thin gold dog leash attached and hanging between her breasts.

Carly tried not to stare but her eyes were drawn to the deep cleavage revealed by the woman's low-cut blouse, with the gold leash nestled prettily between them. The woman stood quietly near the stage, her head bowed, her hands clasped loosely in front of her.

There were rows of chairs set up facing the stage and people were taking their seats. Carly glanced at her watch and slipped into one of the back rows. She didn't know what to expect but a little thrill of excitement was bubbling up inside her nonetheless.

It was as if she was embarking on a whole new life. The persona of steady reliable working woman had shifted. She was metamorphosing into something new, something different and exciting. For the first time in her life, Carly was taking risks.

Her attention was captured by a man who looked to be in his late twenties, with dark wavy hair curling around a face with finely chiseled features. He had rich brown eyes the color of dark chocolate and a full, sensual mouth. He looked Native American or Hispanic, or some mixture of the two, with a creamy toffee-colored complexion and a strong jaw. He wasn't tall, maybe only five-foot-ten, but his bearing was regal, even commanding. He was dressed simply in jeans and a black long-sleeved T-shirt. He wore dark brown boots under his jeans that looked soft and well-worn. Carly couldn't help but notice how cute his butt looked packed into his close-fitting jeans.

She shifted in her seat, suddenly uncomfortable with her own strong response to this man. She noticed everyone was sitting now, quieting as the man walked up onto the stage and adjusted a microphone stand. The lights in the room were suddenly dimmed and the lights on the stage were turned up, drawing everyone's attention to it.

The lovely woman with the dog leash still stood quietly by the stage, now in shadow. She hadn't moved a muscle as he had walked past her.

"Good evening, everyone." The man's voice wasn't deep, but more of a warm baritone, smooth like creamy butter. Carly wanted to hear it again. He obliged. "My name is Jesse Hernandez. I'll be running the seminar tonight." He paused, looking out at the small room.

"I see some familiar faces, and welcome you. I also see some people I don't recognize and I want to welcome you as well." Carly crossed her legs, looking away. It seemed as if he was looking right at her! She felt a flush on her skin and she licked her lips, wondering if he really was looking at her, if he could even see her with the bright lights trained on him as they were. Probably not. She looked back at him.

"Tonight we'll focus on some basic techniques. First, I want to talk about whips. How to choose them, what to look for." He stepped back to a long table Carly hadn't noticed before. On it were a number of whips and floggers. Jesse lifted one after the other as he talked about what to look for when purchasing a whip, including the quality of the leather, the skill of the craftsmanship, the weight of the handle, the feel of it in your hand, the appeal to the eye.

He talked about different types of floggers, whips, crops and single lashes, lifting different items from the table as he spoke. Throughout the demonstration he emphasized the importance of trust and communication in a good D/s relationship. Finally he said, "And now, a demonstration in technique. Angela?"

The woman who had been waiting as still as a statue glided up the stairs, her head still bowed. She stood quietly next to Jesse as he lectured briefly about the "art" of a good whipping.

"When you whip your sub, it isn't about punishment. Or it shouldn't be. The whip is an instrument of passion. A way of expressing your sensual connection with your sub. It isn't about pain or torture. It's about the intensely personal connection that can be achieved when consensual partners share in this profound exchange.

"I know that sounds lofty and poetic, but really it's the essence of a D/s relationship or it should be. Now, Angela is going to help me show you what I mean. She is going to pick the implement for her whipping and she is going to submit with grace as she always does. Aren't you, Angela?"

The room was perfectly still as the woman nodded and turned toward the table. She selected a large flogger of deep burgundy red. The thirty or so tails were braided together in strands of three. Kneeling gracefully before the man, she held the whip on upturned palms, her head bowed.

It was as if everyone in the room was holding their collective breath, including Carly. She watched in fascination as the man stepped behind the woman on stage and touched her head with his fingertips. Angela immediately bent forward so her forehead rested on the stage, her dark auburn hair spilling around her, obscuring her face.

Even from the back row where Carly sat, she could see the woman's bottom was bare, the miniskirt now riding up to reveal pale globes. The woman was facing to the side but even so, it seemed she wasn't wearing any underwear. Carly noticed many of the men were shifting in their seats, no doubt trying to unobtrusively adjust their sudden erections.

Jesse brought the whip down against Angela's bared ass and the swish of leather making contact resounded in the silent room. Carly jumped at the sound, her eyes riveted to the scene. Angela didn't move at all as Jesse continued to whip her, all the while continuing his lecture on technique in a casual tone.

Carly wished she could see Angela's face. Did it hurt? Was she crying? How did she stay so still! She tuned into Jesse's monologue as he was saying, "A volunteer, perhaps? Would someone like to come up and try this riding crop?"

He had set down the heavy whip and picked up a long, black, thin rod with a thick shiny square of leather at its tip. Jesse spoke for a moment about how to hold the crop to make the "prettiest mark" without damaging the skin. He peered out at the audience, looking past a few waving hands toward the back, toward Carly.

Carly looked down, her face burning. There was no way she was going to volunteer to whip that woman! She'd start in the privacy of her own "playroom" on Monday, not in front of fifty people, all of whom knew much more than she!

"Okay, Peter. Looks like you're the lucky volunteer. Come on up."

A lanky man of about fifty years stood up and shuffled his way past the others in his row. As he climbed the stairs of the stage Jesse tapped Angela's shoulder and she lifted her head, turning her face for a moment to the audience. Carly had expected to see tears but what she saw surprised her.

Angela's expression could only be called rapturous. She was flushed, her lips parted, her eyes shining as if she'd just had a heavenly vision. Her hair framed her face like a halo. Jesse took her hand, helping her to stand. Her little skirt was still scrunched up at her waist, revealing the fact she was actually wearing a matching red leather thong that covered her mons but completely revealed her rounded cheeks.

Slowly she turned for the audience, showing them her ass marked with a crisscross of red lines. She remained in that position, her back to the room. *Surely she must be in pain*, Carly thought, and yet again the woman stood perfectly still, her posture relaxed but proud.

Now the man called Peter approached her holding the riding crop in his hand. He struck her without preamble and Angela jerked forward a little bit. Jesse commented quietly, "Perhaps not quite so hard to start with. Warm her up. And remember her skin is sensitive now from the flogger."

Peter grunted but his next blow was softer. He struck her several times on the same spot and Carly could see it reddening. The leather flap produced a slapping sound that jarred her ear, unlike the almost hypnotic swish of sound when the many strands of leather were raining down on soft flesh. Angela had begun to move from side to side and her soft moans were picked up by the microphone.

Jesse watched for a moment more and then put his hand on Peter's wrist, saying firmly, "Thank you, Peter. I'll take over now." Peter didn't seem to want to stop. He managed to get in one final especially savage blow, which elicited a cry from Angela.

As Peter ambled off the stage, his expression smug, Jesse turned to the audience. "You can see from that little demonstration there are different approaches to the art of domination. Peter here obviously prefers the rough approach— seeing how much the sub can take before they fall out of position or beg for mercy. For some slaves this is the perfect approach. They derive as much satisfaction from this kind of treatment as the Dom derives from delivering it. I guess the key here is knowing your sub."

He leaned over now, whispering something in Angela's ear. She nodded and adjusted her skirt to cover her bottom. Gracefully she left the stage, her head again bowed. Jesse continued, facing his audience. "Angela is not into pain per se. She takes a whipping beautifully as you observed, and it will even make her fly. Flying," he said as an aside, "for all you newbies, is the altered state one can achieve when pain and pleasure truly combine. I haven't personally experienced it, but subs have told me it's a spiritual place where sensuality and deep peace are wrought into something more powerful than mere sexual experience. Almost makes you want to be a masochist, doesn't it?"

A few chuckles from the audience as he continued. "At any rate, as I was saying, Angela doesn't get off on pain for its own sake. She favors what I call a 'sensual' whipping. She responds more to the loving kiss of the lash than to the smack of the crop."

"So why'd you call me up there, Hernandez? She's a slave—she should take what she's given. She's submissive. She has to submit to whatever her Dom metes out." Peter's voice was a loud, deep bass, echoing in the small room. Peter, again seated, apparently felt he was being judged and found wanting by the speaker.

Jesse answered, "I agree with you to a point, Peter. When Angela volunteered for this session, she knew she might not be getting just exactly what pleased her. And I did ask you up here because I know you favor the crop. I appreciate there are different styles and I think you provided us with an apt demonstration of that fact.

"This isn't a science—more of an art. But I adamantly disagree with your remark about subs *having* to submit to whatever's 'meted out' by a Dom. That's a common misperception by people not in the scene. That just because a woman, or man for that matter, has submissive feelings and needs, she or he is *required* to submit to whatever whims some Dominant has. As I said before, it's about communication and trust. If you force your will on someone, it's no longer consensual—it's bullying."

As Peter reddened Jesse added, smiling a little, "I know you didn't mean it like that, Peter. I know you would never force yourself on anyone like that. You have too much class for that sort of behavior."

Peter grunted again, his expression indicating he wasn't sure if he'd been complimented or insulted.

Jesse sat down on the front edge of the stage, holding a give and take with the audience, answering questions and giving his opinions about domination and submission.

Carly listened raptly, absorbing it all while at the same time not quite believing it was true. Did people actually "own" one another? Did it go beyond mere playing at kinky BDSM clubs? Did it go beyond posturing at these basement clubs? These people were talking about their "slaves" but she could glean from the context they meant their lovers. Did people really live like this 24/7?

The formal part of the meeting was over and people were again standing and mingling, talking in little groups. Several people had joined Jesse on stage to examine his table of whips, floggers and crops.

Carly watched the man for a while, admiring his easy grace as he talked to the other people. She didn't see Angela anywhere. She found herself wondering if Angela "belonged" to Jesse Hernandez. Was she his slave? His lover?

Carly refused to admit she might be a little jealous at the thought. What was he to her? She didn't date perverts! She was just here to learn. Job training, that's all this was. She stood up and grabbed her purse, planning to slip out before anyone tried to approach her.

As she was almost out the door Jake Mitchell was suddenly beside her. He put his hand on her arm, forcing her to stop and acknowledge him. "So, what'd ya' think? How would you like to be whipped with that flogger? Hernandez is the guy to do it. Especially with a newbie like you. He'd make you cry tears of joy."

Carly pulled her arm away, embarrassed and annoyed. "I *told* you. I'm a Domme! Not a sub." How easily she used the terms, she thought suddenly and she smiled.

Jake mistook her smile as one of friendliness and said, "Yeah, yeah, sure you are, babe. Listen, you don't have to hide anything here. We're all close here. Just because you Dom folks for a living, that doesn't make you *Domme*. It's just a job. Of course, I guess it helps if you're really into it, but I doubt many pros really are. Am I right?"

Like I would know, Carly thought. But she answered, "I suppose you're right. But anyway, thanks for the seminar. I really do have to be going now."

"So soon? I was hoping to get a chance to introduce myself."

The voice wasn't Jake Mitchell's. It was Jesse Hernandez who had come up behind them. Carly turned toward him, startled. She hadn't expected to suddenly be so close to the handsome man. Somehow his being on the stage had made him bigger than life in her mind and now she took a moment to get her arms around the idea he was just a guy, standing about two feet from her, his hand extended in greeting.

"Jesse Hernandez," he said unnecessarily.

"Carly. Carly Stevens."

"A pleasure to meet you." He held her hand just a second too long. Carly was the first to pull away. She held the hand he had touched with her other hand. It must have been her imagination but it felt hot to the touch.

"How did you like the seminar? Learn anything?"

"Oh, it was, um, very informative. I'm a professional Dominatrix over at Club de Sade and—"

"No kidding. So you know Amanda Merritt?"

"Well, no, I haven't actually met her. That is, I'm just starting over there next week, actually. I know Anthony."

Jesse smiled, perhaps not noticing her blush at being caught out pretending to more experience than she had. "Ah, Anthony. Such a *dear* boy." Jesse spoke the last sentence with just the affected tone Anthony himself used, causing Carly to laugh.

Jesse took her arm, moving her away from Jake who had shown no sign of leaving the two of them alone. He led her to one of the tables set up near the juice bar. "Sorry, just wanted to get away from Jake there. He's a nice enough guy but if you give him an inch, he'll take a mile. He'll talk your ear off, informing you all about yourself whether you want to hear it or not."

"It's funny you should say that. He was trying to tell me I was a sub! He doesn't even know me." Carly laughed, throwing her head back as if this was the most amusing thing in the world. Even as she was doing it, she knew she was putting on a show for this man. She stopped laughing abruptly and blushed again, turning her head away.

Jesse watched her, making no comment. Softly he said, "Have you ever been whipped, Carly?"

"No! Of course not! I told you," she doggedly reiterated, "I'm a Domme. A professional Dominatrix."

"Yes, so you said. You know what my theory is on that? I think all Doms should experience the whip. The cane. The single lash. Cuffs, chains, piercing, branding, wax, whatever it is they intend to inflict on their sub. If you're willing to do it to someone else, my personal feeling is you should know just what exactly it is you're demanding."

Carly was quiet, taking this in. It made a certain sense, she supposed. As she processed all of what he had just said she blurted, "Caning? Piercing? Branding? Jeeze, do you guys really *do* that stuff? Is it even legal?"

Jesse laughed a rich deep laugh. "If by 'you guys' you mean Doms, of which you just finished assuring me you are one, well, yes, we guys really do that. Not everyone, obviously. I was talking in extremes but it's certainly out there." He looked directly at Carly, his dark brown eyes seeming to penetrate her secret thoughts. She found herself staring back even though she wanted to look away.

"Tell me truthfully, Carly. How much experience do you really have? No offense, but you strike me as rather new to all this. The way you were watching the demo, your eyes as wide as a kid's—"

"You could see me?" Carly flushed and bit her lip. So she'd been right after all. How embarrassing!

"Sure. Though I have to admit, I was especially looking. When you walked in, I caught sight of you and made a mental note to find you after the seminar."

"Why?"

Now Jesse looked a little embarrassed. "Well, you are a very attractive woman. Sexy and cute at the same time. You remind me of Meg Ryan, actually."

Carly grinned. She'd been told this before, many times, but it still pleased her. She was surprised Jesse Hernandez was interested in her. She said as much. "Wait, aren't you with Angela? I mean, don't you, um, own her?" She felt silly saying this but didn't know how else to put it.

"Angela?" Jesse paused a moment as if he was trying to figure out what she meant. "Oh, because I whipped her? No. No, of course not. That was just for demonstration purposes. Nothing between us."

As Carly looked confused he went on. "I'm sorry. I forget you don't know the players. This really is a pretty small community. I mean, once you get into the serious stuff like seminars and public scenes. Angela is famous, at least in BDSM circles. She belongs to Frank Channing. She's 'on loan' tonight, if you will. Frank would have been here himself but he had to be on call at the hospital. By day he's a doctor, by night a 'wild and crazy' Dom. They practically live on the club circuit. They're out just about every night and Angela is very popular entertainment for the crowds, as you might imagine. She really gets off on public displays of her submission and Frank digs it, too. Whatever floats your boat, right?"

"Huh," Carly said, absorbing it all. "I guess so, yeah."

"But you avoided the question, young lady. How much experience do you really have in the scene? Why are you here tonight?"

Why keep up the charade? She didn't know this man, though she realized as she thought this she'd like to know him better. Feeling a little stupid because of her earlier claims she admitted, "Well, actually I have no experience. Zippo. Zilch. I just quit my job without having anything else lined up and my girlfriend found this want ad for this Dominatrix thing and I called and the guy said come down and bam! I had the job!"

Jesse laughed. Carly had begun by speaking at a normal speed but it had gotten faster and faster as the words tumbled out. He said, "So now you have this job under false pretenses and you have to hurry and learn what the hell to do before they find out and fire your butt, am I right?"

"Right as rain, unfortunately," she said ruefully.

"Well, did you get anything out of tonight's demonstration?"

"I did actually."

"Tell me honestly, not what you learned about technique or what whips to buy, but how did it make you *feel*? Were you horrified? Intrigued? Turned on?"

"A little of each I guess. I was actually a little surprised at my own reactions."

"What do you mean? Tell me." He was so focused on her, so attentive. No surreptitious glance at his watch, no looking around the room as she spoke. He seemed genuinely interested in what she had to say. And she didn't get the feeling he was putting any sexual moves on her either—not that she'd have minded! He just seemed to really want to know her opinions on what she'd experienced. He was easy to talk to and she felt cared for, somehow. It wasn't a feeling she was used to.

"Well. I felt kind of scared in a way. Scared for Angela, afraid you were going to hurt her. But then I could see how intense it was for her. Her face when she turned toward us. It was like those faces in the medieval icons of the Virgin Mary or something. A kind of almost religious rapture lit up her features. It was really something to see. I mean—" Carly leaned forward, unaware of her short springy blonde hair falling forward, making her look suddenly very young "—it was so obvious she wasn't *suffering*. I think I had this mental picture this was all about torture. About inflicting pain. Sadistically hurting someone and deriving pleasure from that. But that isn't at all what she experienced. That was obvious."

"You expressed that well," Jesse said, nodding. "You seem to have a real connection with the submissive mentality, even if you are Domme," he added, grinning. Now he did glance at his watch. "Damn, I have to go. I have to be somewhere. Listen—" he put his hand on Carly's arm but the gesture was gentle "—I've really enjoyed connecting with you. Do you think we might, uh, meet again? I mean, that is, if you're not, um, involved…"

As he sputtered to a halt Carly smiled. Was he asking her out? This sexy, confident man was suddenly acting like a teenage boy terrified of rejection at a school dance. His trepidation gave her confidence she wouldn't otherwise have had. "I'd love to meet again," she said sincerely, realizing it was true. It wasn't just his drop-dead gorgeous looks that attracted her or his ability to captivate a crowd with his public speaking, but a genuine feeling of friendship that seemed to have blossomed between them in just the few short minutes they had spoken together.

Jesse smiled broadly and his dark eyes seemed to sparkle. His teeth were large and even against his smooth tanned skin. Carly was a sucker for good teeth and she smiled back. Jesse took out a thin black wallet from his back pocket and extracted a business card. Carly accepted it, feeling a little thrill as his fingers lightly touched hers. *Jesse Hernandez, Private Investigator* it read, with an address and phone number listed below.

"Wow, a private investigator!" Carly said, impressed. "So you're not a professional Dom, huh?"

"Well, I don't work in a club, if that's what you mean. I am dominant by nature, yes, but I don't make a living at it. There isn't too much call for professional male Doms, at least not straight ones. Women don't have to pay for it generally. There are plenty of guys out there just dying to do it for free."

He grinned but then added seriously, "Anyway, I wouldn't want to do that. It's too special to me. For me D/s is a romantic connection between two people. I do these seminars because I've seen so much crap and posturing 'in the scene'. I've seen so many wannabe assholes who think because they can buy a whip and order some girl around they are 'Dom'.

"Often it turns out really they're just insecure bullies who use the whole BDSM scene as a way to act out their aggressive feelings toward women and to mask their inadequacies as a man. I can't stand people like that. I'll expose them whenever I see them. Life is too short for that kind of bullshit."

Carly nodded, thinking it over. She hadn't given any thought to what it really entailed to be Dominant or submissive in a relationship. She was beginning to suspect the club scene and her job as a "professional Dominatrix" really had little to do with real D/s relationships between partners.

"You've given me a lot to think about," she said honestly.

Jesse looked sheepish and added, "Hey, I'm sorry. I certainly didn't mean to imply there's anything wrong with making a buck. You offer a service men want. Lecture over. I get on this soapbox and I know I can be a bore. Worse than Jake!"

They both glanced over to the burly man who was gesticulating with both hands at two women who looked as if they were seeking a quick means of retreat, backing slowly away from him as he edged forward, apparently oblivious to their response.

Carly laughed and shook her head. "Not at all! I really appreciate the time you've spent with me. I'm not sure about this whole club thing. I mean, Anthony assured me it was legal but—"

"Oh, it's legal. You're not peddling sex, at least not directly, so the city of New York is okay with it. You have specific guidelines to follow and as long as there's—" Carly chimed in unison with him as he said "—no exchange of bodily fluids," and they both laughed. "Well, yeah. It's pretty much becomes like a massage parlor—no sex but lots of touching. They watch you though, so be careful. Stick by the rules and you should be fine."

Carly glanced at her watch. "But you said you had to go?"

"Oh, you made me forget the time!" Jesse stood up and extended his hand. "It was really terrific meeting you, Carly. Good luck with this pro thing. Call me if you need some pointers. Oh! I almost forgot!" He pulled out another business card and set it down on the table in front of Carly, along with a black ballpoint pen.

Again he looked a little shy as he said, "For you to write your number. If you want to, that is. I mean, if you'd rather just call me that's cool." He slapped his forehead suddenly and groaned. "Oh, shit. You've probably got a boyfriend! What am I thinking? A gorgeous woman like you!"

Carly was flattered but she grinned and admitted, "Nope. Not a one. Can't say as I do. No attachments. Free as a bird." She laughed a little, realizing she sounded like an idiot but unable to stop. She picked up the pen and scrawled her name and phone number across it.

"Ah, a lefty I see," Jesse observed.

"Yep," Carly quipped. "A sign of genius."

"Uh-huh, whatever you say," Jesse answered.

They grinned goofily at each other a moment or two before Carly said, "Where are you off to? Solving a murder?" As soon as Carly spoke she wished she hadn't asked. She didn't know him well enough yet—he might think she was prying. What if he was off to meet his lover? He hadn't said *he* didn't have a girlfriend! Silently she cursed herself.

But Jesse answered easily. "No, actually it's a lot more mundane than that. I rarely get involved in murder investigations. Usually it's finding missing persons, trailing guys who are messing around on their wives and tracking down insurance fraud. Tonight I'm tailing a guy who is supposed to be attending a late business meeting in Newark but his wife thinks he's really meeting his girlfriend at a ritzy hotel. It's not my favorite work—this kind of spouse-spying stuff, but it's easy and it pays pretty good."

"Well," Carly said, pocketing his business card as he slipped the one she'd written on into his pocket, "now I know who to call if I need some private investigating!"

"Let's hope you never do," Jesse said as they headed together toward the door. "How about I walk you to your car?"

"Seeing as I don't own one, that'll be tough." Carly grinned. "But you can walk me to my subway stop if you want."

"It's a deal." They managed to sidestep Jake Mitchell as he headed purposefully toward them, no doubt eager to hold forth.

"That was a close one," Carly laughed as they slipped through the exit and stepped together into the clear night.

Chapter Four

80

"This is the code." Anthony and Carly were standing just inside the door of Club de Sade on a bright October afternoon, the first day of Carly's new career. Though she didn't have any clients scheduled yet, he'd asked her to come in for any "walk-ins" and to get all her paperwork filed.

Anthony punched in a series of four numbers and said, "It's Amanda's dog's birthday. She's nuts for that dog. You'll probably get to meet her later if she comes around. Amanda, not her dog," he grinned.

"Now, the alarm is always set because you can't be too careful in the big, bad city. You just have to use your key and then step in, flip open this little box and punch in the code." He demonstrated again and then said, "There, I just activated the alarm. Now you deactivate it. That's what you'll do when you come in. Then you'll reset it once you close the door again. It's easy."

Carly pressed the buttons — five, one, nine, nine — and the little box beeped as a light on the corner glowed green. "Good. Now set it again and it'll be on." Carly obeyed and the light glowed a blinking red.

"Perfect." As they walked into the library just off the front door Anthony added, "Clients ring the doorbell and I check them out via short-circuit camera." He pointed to a small black and white TV screen in the corner of the room connected to a camera set up outside. Carly could see an image of the front door and stoop. She recalled ringing the bell when she had come for her interview, unaware he must have checked her out first.

"There's a back entrance off the kitchen, too. Same setup, same code back there, though no camera. Nobody uses it much though. Dark alleys! Ugh!"

The doorbell rang and Anthony glanced at his watch and then at the TV screen. He sighed and said, "Jolene's first client is here and she's late as usual. Where is that girl! I'll have to get the door! I am so sick of hopping up and down. I can't get anything done between the phone and the door. I really need a receptionist. I'm so behind on the books it's ridiculous. I've told Amanda a hundred times we need to hire someone. I think she's about to come around. Meanwhile, I can barely keep my head above water!" As if to prove him right the phone rang.

"Shit!" Anthony expostulated. "Can you get the door? I'll just be a second. I know the guy—it's okay. Just show him into the parlor and tell him Mistress Jolene will be right with him." Without waiting for her to agree, Anthony turned toward his phone and picked up the receiver. "Club de Sade. Anthony at your service."

Carly wanted to protest but didn't dare. How big a deal was it to answer the door, anyway? She worked here now, didn't she? She hadn't changed yet into her "scene" outfit, not wanting to travel on the bus in leather and stiletto heels. She was dressed in jeans and a dark blue blouse with sneakers on her feet and no makeup on her face. She looked much more like a teenager than a slave-driving mistress. She felt more like one, too.

The doorbell rang again and Carly hurried out to the foyer. "Don't forget the alarm," Anthony called out. Carly flipped open the little door of the alarm box and punched in the numbers of Amanda's dog's birthday. The alarm beeped its approval and she turned to the door, unlocking and opening it.

A very tall, plump man with a body shaped like a pear stood in the doorway. He started to smile but the smile shifted to uncertainty and it was clear Carly wasn't who he was expecting. He clutched a small leather suitcase protectively in front of his groin. "Oh," he said in a deep voice, "*You* aren't Mistress Jolene. Where's my mistress?" His tone was almost petulant.

Carly, trying to sound calm and commanding as she imagined a Dominatrix might, answered, "Mistress Jolene commands you to wait in the parlor. She'll come get you when she's ready." She hoped she sounded convincing. She'd been reading up on this sort of thing online, trying to research the psyche of the submissive man, whatever that might be.

From what she could glean, submissive men and submissive women weren't all that different. From various testimonials and journals she had read online, they all seemed to be seeking a similar goal—to give themselves over to another person in what appeared to be a consensual exchange of sexual power. In the romantic relationships she'd read about the connection could be very intense, as she recalled Jesse describing a little bit during his lecture.

She tingled a little at the memory of Jesse. He hadn't called her yet. Probably full of shit like every handsome, sexy guy she met. But then she hadn't called him either. It was the twenty-first century after all. A woman could pick up the phone and call a guy. Yet she hated to do it—it made her seem needy and grasping, she thought. She wanted the guy to be the one to make the first move. Not very modern of her, she supposed, but there it was.

She looked at the man standing passively before her, his expression no longer petulant but tinged with respect, the little case now held easily at his side. She had gotten the impression from her limited research the sort of men who frequented these fetish clubs often enjoyed being treated roughly—humiliated and insulted as a part of their turn-on.

"Mistress will see you when she's good and ready. Where are your manners, slave?" The "slave" just slipped off Carly's tongue and for a moment she was afraid she'd gone too far. The fellow just grinned, however. Her answer seemed to satisfy him and he dutifully followed Carly into the parlor. "Pardon me, ma'am," he atoned as he set his leather case down on the coffee table.

"Wait here," she again commanded, feeling a small thrill as she ordered this big man about.

"On the furniture?" he whispered, seemingly aghast.

It took Carly a second to understand what he meant. Hoping she had it right she snapped, "Of course not on the furniture, slave! Kneel on the floor where you belong!"

"Yes, Mistress," the man breathed reverentially, sinking to the floor with surprising grace for a man his size and girth.

Carly couldn't suppress a grin as she nodded in what she hoped was an imperious manner. "I'll let your mistress know you're here." She realized she had forgotten to reset the alarm and hurried over to the door to input the code once again.

She walked back to the library where Anthony was just hanging up. "We're up shit creek, as usual. That was Jolene. Called in sick. *Again.*" He rolled his eyes in an exaggerated gesture, which led Carly to understand this was something Jolene did often. "She says she *forgot* about Tommy boy out there and now here he sits, waiting for his session with no mistress to serve."

As Carly stood still, Anthony's eyes slid over her. "Wait a minute. What am I thinking? We have you! Mistress Carly. No, no. That won't do. You don't want to use your real name. Let's see. What's a good name for you?" He squinted at her, one hand massaging his chin as he pondered the question.

"Mistress Marlena! How about that? It's exotic and European. They'll eat it up. You like it?"

"Yes, I guess so. I mean, if you say so." Carly stood uncertain. Was he suggesting she take this man, this client, this "Tommy boy" and Dom him? Now? She swallowed and said, "You want me to take this client? Jolene's client?"

"Sure, why not? Everything you need is upstairs. Take the blue room. That's where Mistress Jolene usually takes Tommy. All her whips and stuff are up there." It's the last room on the right." He looked at her sharply. "Where's your stuff? Did you bring your own toys?" He peered at the duffel bag she had brought in with her when she had first arrived.

"Um, I wanted to get some new things. I don't really have much I want to use."

"You've got an outfit, right? Some decent makeup? You're going to lose the fresh-faced Barbie doll look, right? These guys don't go for that."

"Of course I do!" Carly felt affronted. Did he take her for a total idiot?

"Well, good. You can use the house toys. God knows we have plenty. You may want to add your own favorites, of course, as you get more comfortable here. Meanwhile, go get changed and I'll handle Tommy for a few minutes. I'll bring him up to you."

He rifled through a file cabinet drawer and withdrew a slim folder. "Here're the stats on Tommy. His likes and tastes. It's not exhaustive but it'll do in a pinch." He handed the folder to Carly and said, "Go on. You can change upstairs. There's a bathroom right next to the blue room. I'll send Tommy up to you in about ten minutes. Unless he balks, of course, in which case I'll kill myself and then Jolene, not in that order."

The doorbell rang and they both turned to the screen, where a young man of medium height stood nervously, his hands clasped in front of him. "That's Mistress Ava's boy. She'd better—"

Whatever he was going to say was cut off by a cigarette-graveled voice as a large woman of about forty-five stuck her head in the library and said, "Chill your bones, Anthony. Mistress Ava has arrived with bells on to serve her adoring clientele." She was dressed in a long black velvet evening gown that revealed much of her ample bosom.

Carly couldn't help but stare at her cleavage. Mistress Ava laughed a deep-throated chuckle and said, "You must be Carly. The new girl Anthony can't stop talking about. I didn't know we were hiring children now." Her voice was a mixture of disdain and amusement.

Anthony intervened. "She's *not* a child." His tone was haughty, as if Ava had personally insulted him. "This is *Mistress Marlena*. And don't let looks deceive you. She's an experienced Dominatrix with extensive experience. She's just going to change now and take Tommy. Jolene's flaked out again."

Ava eyed Carly dubiously but didn't argue the point. Instead she said, "Well, the red room's mine when I'm here. Guess you'll be in blue?" As Carly nodded, Ava said, "Off to collect my slave boy." She departed with a flourish.

The phone rang again and with an exasperated sigh, Anthony reached for it. "Club de Sade. Anthony at your service." While listening to the caller, Anthony looked up at Carly who was still standing in front of him holding the manila folder with the facts on "Tommy".

"Go on, go on," Anthony mouthed silently, waving his hand in a dismissive gesture. Carly turned and went, taking her large duffel bag with her. She slipped past the parlor and up the stairs. One door was shut but she could hear muffled voices within as she passed. Mistress Ava and her boy toy, no doubt. She walked down the length of the hall. With no windows and the light not yet switched on, the hallway was gloomy and filled with shadows. She almost tripped against the large old potted plant that stood just beside the last door.

The door was ajar and she pushed it all the way open, peering in. This room had a large window on one wall, which let in the light, now waning in the late afternoon. The room was aptly named, as it was indeed painted blue, a pale robin's egg blue on the walls with darker blue trim and molding. It contained one of the famous "torture chairs" as well as an assortment of whips and crops hanging from hooks along one wall. There was also a neat coil of rope, some candles and matches and several long rather sharp looking knives. These items were laid out neatly on a high narrow table against one wall.

Carly stared at the knives, remembering Anthony's remarks about knife play. *It takes all kinds*, she thought, but then admonished herself. Who was she to judge? She was about to dress up in leather and do God knows what to the big, fat fellow waiting patiently in the parlor.

After shutting the door, Carly kicked off her sneakers and tucked her socks neatly into them. Quickly she stripped off her blouse and jeans, pulling on the smooth soft black leather pants that fit her supple lean legs like a second skin. After a moment's hesitation she took off her bra — the vest looked better without it, she knew.

Hurriedly she folded her clothing into her duffel and tossed it into the closet, which was empty except for a few stray hangars and some extra blankets piled on a shelf. Sitting on the bed she pulled on her stiletto boots, feeling like some kind of delicious villain in a comic book.

There was a large mirror hung on the wall opposite the "torture chair" — no doubt to enhance the experience for the victim. Carly stood in front of the mirror to apply her makeup, adding a golden pink eye shadow, dark kohl lining and dark mascara. She chose a red lipstick and then stood back, eyeing herself critically in the mirror.

She had to admit the effect was pretty stunning! The so-called fresh-faced Barbie was now a rather daunting-looking mistress, if she said so herself! Her breasts, not large by today's augmented standards, were nevertheless a nice thirty-four C. They were pressed alluringly together by the tight leather vest. Feeling daring, Carly unzipped it just a little more so fully half of her creamy breasts were revealed.

The high-heeled boots added a good four inches to her height, which made her feel rather grand. Hopefully she could walk in them without wobbling! She wanted to make a good impression with her very first client! Remembering the folder, she took it from the bed where she had set it down to change and, perching again on the edge of the bed, she opened it.

The text was written in large girlish printing with red ink. It read *Tommy, Likes — verbal humiliation — especially dog play, light bondage, foot worship, spanking with hand and hairbrush. Dislikes — whipping, severe beating, total nudity.*

It wasn't much to go by, but Carly was relieved to see at least Tommy didn't plan on getting totally naked and also she wouldn't have to use the whip her first time out. What the heck was dog play? Hopefully she could wing it. Maybe even get a few pointers from the client himself, as part of his "training".

A sound in the hall made her start. She heard voices, this time both male, as Anthony was leading her first client down the hall.

This is it! she thought excitedly, feeling equal parts dread and anticipation. She took a deep breath as she struck a pose — hands on her hips, her chin raised in what she hoped was a dominant attitude. There was a knock upon the door.

"Come in," she said in a loud and, she hoped, confident voice.

The door opened and in walked Anthony, leading Tommy by a dog leash. Anthony held the man's bag, which he put down on the floor as he jerked at the leash.

"Down, boy!" Anthony said in a stern voice. Tommy stood in only his boxers and a thick leather collar decorated with silver studs. In his mouth he held a large plastic hairbrush. His body was pink and mostly hairless, almost feminine with rounded shoulders and broad hips.

As the large man dropped obediently to all fours Anthony turned to Carly, winking at her as he said, "Mistress Marlena, I've explained to Tommy here that Mistress Jolene is displeased with him and has sent you to punish him for his bad behavior. I've brought this newspaper for you to whack his naughty bottom. Don't forget to set your timer."

Before she could respond Anthony was out the door, pulling it closed behind him. She could dimly hear a phone ringing and assumed he was running to get it. Left alone with Tommy, Carly took a deep breath and sat on the edge of the bed.

Tommy hadn't moved, his head down, his large body still. "Dog!" she shouted and he jerked a little. Carly realized he still held the hairbrush between his teeth. She reached down and took it from him, setting it down on the night table. The handle was wet from his doggy grip. She closed her eyes and willed herself to let "Mistress Marlena" channel through her. She could do this!

She turned the dial on the little timer as she demanded, "Answer me! Have you been a bad dog? Did you mess up your mistress's new rug?" Would he go for it?

He did. "Yes, Mistress. I've been a very bad dog. I need to be punished."

"Yes, you do, you bad, bad dog." Carly stood and took the rolled newspaper Anthony had thoughtfully provided. She walked behind the man and tentatively whacked his boxer-clad bottom with it. He didn't move. She hit him harder, as hard as she could.

"Thank you, Mistress!" he gasped, wiggling his bottom slightly, clearly asking for more. She obliged, smacking him again and again until her arm was tired. This was kind of silly, but at least it was easy.

"Are you sorry, you bad dog?" she demanded.

"Yes, Mistress!" Tommy replied. He was breathing heavily.

"Kneel up," Carly commanded. "Let me look at you." Tommy obeyed and Carly observed his boxers contained a very erect penis that looked as if it was trying to poke its way through the fabric. At least he clearly approved of what was happening. Hopefully she could come up with fifty more minutes of "entertainment" for her client.

"Show me your paces, dog. I'm going to throw this brush—" she grabbed the large hairbrush "—and you will fetch it for me. Let's see what you can do." She tossed the brush a few feet away and Tommy scrambled after it. He grabbed the handle with his mouth and crawled to her feet, holding it up much like a real dog would, his arms crocked in front of him like paws, his expression eager. Carly took the brush, patted him on his balding head and tossed the brush again. Over and over she sent him scurrying to retrieve it. The man showed no signs of tiring of the game.

After several minutes of this Carly said, "You fetch well, but you're still a bad little dog. I'll still have to punish you for Mistress Jolene. You know that, don't you?"

"Oh, yes ma'am," Tommy breathed, adoration shining in his eyes. He actually licked his lips as he eyed her cleavage. Carly felt a curious surge of power and it wasn't unpleasant.

"Very well. Get up. How does Mistress Jolene spank that bad doggy butt?"

"She cuffs my paws, Mistress, because I'm such a disobedient puppy. And she gags me, too, because I might try to bite her. I really am a very bad, very dangerous dog." He grinned, his teeth long and yellow and Carly could well believe it. She experienced a moment's trepidation, but felt in her gut this man was completely harmless. And Anthony was only a phone call away.

Walking over to the toy table, she selected some leather cuffs with silver clips dangling from a little loop in the center of each. Tommy obediently held out his wrists. Carly pressed the Velcro closures shut though she didn't yet clip them together. Turning back toward the table, she didn't see any gags. Tommy seemed to read her mind because he offered, "My ball gag is in my bag, Mistress. Shall I get it for you?"

Of course—clients wouldn't share gags! That would be unsanitary. "Yes, Tommy dog. Get your gag. I can't have a nasty dog slobbering on me while he gets his spanking!"

Tommy scrambled over to his bag, using his "paws" to open it and retrieve a bright red ball with leather straps and buckles dangling from it. "Shall I put it on, Mistress?"

"Of course!" Carly snapped, relieved he had offered since all those buckles and straps looked confusing. Tommy knelt up to strap his own gag in place and again Carly noted his huge erection, the tip now peeking out of the front flap of his underpants.

When he was done securing the gag, he obediently placed his hands behind his back. Carly clipped the leather cuffs together. Now what? Did she stand behind him and smack him? That would be awkward. And now that he was gagged she couldn't even ask him for direction under the guise of a command. Luckily he stood up and lumbered awkwardly over to the bed, his bound hands impeding his balance slightly.

He fell across the bed and lay passively, apparently waiting for the sting of the plastic hairbrush on his ample bottom. Carly delivered, smacking his bottom, lightly at first, but building in tempo and intensity. Tommy was still at first, but soon began to move in a kind of spasmodic rhythm, lifting his bottom to meet each blow as he grunted against his gag.

She was both relieved and surprised when the timer bell rang. Tommy, apparently used to it, rolled over at once and sat up, lifting his wrists away from his back so Carly could release the clip that held them. She did so and he immediately began unbuckling his own gag.

"Thank you, Mistress." His face was flushed. She could see a wet stain against the front of his boxers—the man had come while being smacked with the hairbrush. Carly felt at once embarrassed and triumphant.

"I hope I get you next time," he whispered.

Chapter Five

ဢ

"He said he hoped he'd get you next time? Wow, that is so cool! See, I *told* you, you would be a natural!" It was eleven-thirty at night and Carly was exhausted. She was lying in her bed in an oversized T-shirt with the phone pressed to her ear. Eva was on the other end, demanding a blow-by-blow of the first day on the job. She had waited up well past her bedtime to hear all the juicy details.

"So did you," Eva's voice lowered in mock horror, "have to have *sex* with these pervs?"

"No, no of course not. That's illegal, remember? No, after Tommy I had three more clients! I made two-hundred-twenty dollars in one night! It'll be double that once I'm up to full salary! But I'm wiped out! It's exhausting work, it really is."

"Oh, I can just imagine." Eva's voice was sarcastic. "So were the other clients little doggies, too?"

"No. Jimmy was into being tied up in that chair thing and having me slap his face and attach clothespins to his cock and balls."

"What!" Eva exploded, clearly relishing the shocking details. "That is so *sick!*"

"Well, you know, I would have agreed before I started getting into this, but now I'm not so sure. I mean, who's to say what is and isn't 'sick'? If something arouses someone and it doesn't hurt anyone else, who are we to judge?"

"Yeah, especially if they're willing to give you a ton of money to do it!" Eva said, laughing.

Carly laughed, too. It did seem kind of funny now, but when she had had that man strapped naked into the chair completely at her mercy, his cock and shaven balls rigid with arousal, it had been something else altogether.

She thought now about her own reaction. Part fear — would she make a fool of herself? Part excitement — it was erotic to be standing in sexy clothing she knew made her look hot, with a naked man — and this one had been young and handsome, no doubt adding to the allure of the situation — helpless before her. Part thrill — there was a very real rush from having that kind of complete power over someone.

Of course he could stop it at any time by giving whatever prearranged signal they had agreed upon if things became too intense, but for that hour they had suspended reality. He had in fact become her suffering slave boy and she had in fact become his dominating, cruel mistress. It had been a kick. More than that — it had been intense. When he had ejaculated just from the torture, Carly had felt powerful and tender all at once.

Carly found she didn't want to articulate all of this to Eva. Eva would laugh and tease her. Not having experienced it, Eva wouldn't understand. So instead she talked in a lighthearted manner about the other "clients", laughing along with Eva at their particular fetishes.

She yawned elaborately and said, "Well, Eva, now that you've gotten the down and dirty, let's call it a night. I'm really wiped. I'm going to bed. I wish you hadn't stayed up so late yourself! You're going to be exhausted tomorrow."

"Oh, that's okay. I wanted to. I couldn't have waited all the way until tomorrow to hear how it went! I'm so excited for you. It sounds like this could be your calling! Who would have thought? Little Meg Ryan look-alike goody two-shoes ending up a mistress in a den of iniquity."

"Shut up and go to sleep."

When Eva had hung up, Carly lay in her single bed, staring up at the ceiling. Her fingers found their way under the T-shirt as she thought about the amazing evening she had just spent.

How would she feel if someone had tied *her* up and spanked her? Or made her lick their feet and thank them when they smacked her bare ass? Did Jesse do that to his lovers? For his lovers?

Jesse. Carly had tried to avoid thinking about the handsome, sexy man. Why hadn't he called her? She had really thought something had connected between them. Something more than mere small talk. Had she let her own attraction fool her?

Carly couldn't remember the last time a man had grabbed her attention the way Jesse Hernandez had. Most men came on so strong they turned her off. Usually she was already inclined to think the worst of any man who approached her. She rarely gave anyone the benefit of the doubt. Yet with Jesse somehow her defenses had been lowered.

He hadn't been demanding or grasping. She hadn't sensed the underlying desperation some men seemed to give off like an odor. No, if anything, she had been the one feeling a little desperate. Perhaps partially because he seemed so calm and confident, she had felt safe enough to allow herself to be attracted.

Whatever the reason, he had gotten under her skin and now he seemed to permeate her subconscious, drifting up into her thoughts if she wasn't careful. But he hadn't called. It had been six days and not a word. Figured. Typical man. Probably went home to his girlfriend or wife and promptly forgot all about her.

Now as she thought over their conversation—for the thousandth time, he had never out and out said he *didn't* have a girlfriend—only that Angela wasn't his lover. That was probably it—he had someone at home. She should just forget him. She didn't need a man anyway—never had.

As she closed her eyes, Jesse's image drifted uninvited into her mind. Those dark eyes seemed to sparkle somehow with an inner secret she wanted to share. The supple skin, like soft toffee-colored fine leather. She wanted to touch it. To trace his cheekbone, to drop her finger to his lips and feel their full sensual possibility...

Carly moaned softly. Somehow, her left hand had slipped down to her pussy, warm and wet, eager for attention after such a strange and sex-charged night with no one to touch her. As she rubbed herself, she felt the familiar hot pleasure rise inside her. Giving up at least for the moment, she let Jesse fully into her fantasies.

Oddly, or maybe it wasn't so odd, given the way she'd just spent the last several hours, her fantasies involved cuffs and chains, only this time *she* was the one bound and helpless. Jesse, tan and sexy in his black shirt and jeans, was the one in control, taking her, claiming her, making love to her...

Carly fell asleep almost as soon as she orgasmed—her fingers still buried in her hot, little sex.

She awoke bleary-eyed to a persistent ringing. What the heck was that noise? As she came fully conscious she realized it was the telephone. What was it, the crack of dawn? Groping blindly, she grabbed the portable receiver from the bedside table where she'd left it the night before.

"'Lo," she mumbled, her eyes still shut.

"Oh, did I wake you?"

Carly's eyes sprang open as her heart leaped into her throat.

"Oh! No, I mean yes, but that's okay. I should be getting up anyway. What time is it?"

"Good morning to you, too," Jesse said, laughing an easy laugh. "It's nine-forty and my apologies for calling so early. I forgot you're a woman of the night now. I know sometimes those clubs don't really get swinging 'til after nine."

Carly sat up, fully awake now, her heart still thumping sweetly in her chest. "Oh, it's okay, really. I actually fell asleep before midnight. Don't know what got into me to sleep so late."

"Well, I wanted to apologize to you."

"For what?"

"Well, I had asked you if I could call and then I took an out-of-town assignment that took longer than I had anticipated. To make matters worse, I must have left the card with your number on it in the pants I was wearing that night. When I went to try and call you, I couldn't find it. I called the Manhattan directory assistance but there were no Carly Stevens."

"Oh, I'm unlisted. Single woman in the city and all…"

"I figured as much. I certainly don't blame you. Anyway, I just got back this morning. I could have called you at seven a.m. when the plane landed, so just be glad I exercised *some* patience."

Relief washed over Carly like a wave of fresh water. He'd called her! He *was* interested! Nonchalantly she admitted, "I *was* kind of wondering…"

"Well, sure you were. I had asked if I could call, and then I didn't. I felt like a total jerk, believe me. And like I said, I apologize. I was wondering if I could make it up to you? Maybe this evening we could go to dinner?"

"Oh, I wish I could. I'm hosting my first party tonight. Anthony wants me there as 'resident mistress'." She laughed self-consciously.

"Ah, the famous Club de Sade parties. I've actually attended a few of those. Sometimes I give a demonstration. It can get pretty wild." Carly sat up, fully awake now, her heart singing. He'd called her!

"Say," Jesse added. "Since you're busy tonight, how about now? I mean, if you don't already have other plans. Maybe we could get a bite of breakfast. I know this great little Greek diner not far from the Paddler Club, if you didn't mind a dive. They serve a great breakfast."

"That sounds perfect. I'm starving and not really in the mood for the ketchup packets and the carton of skim milk which are about all you'll find in my fridge at the moment." Carly's face hurt she was grinning so hard. He'd called her!

They met at Gus' Diner. As she stepped off the bus, she saw him standing in front of the restaurant. He saw her, too, and gave a little wave. She drew in her breath—he was even better-looking than her memory had recorded, with his dark wavy hair cut long but tucked behind his ears, his large dark brown eyes and the easy smile that lit up his features when he saw her.

Breakfast was wonderful. Over hot buttered corn muffins, homemade sausage and the best fried potatoes she'd ever tasted, they talked about themselves, covering everything from their childhoods to their dreams for the future. Unlike many of the men Carly had dated, Jesse really did seem to want to know all about her, asking questions and actually paying attention to the answers. It made her feel valued and special. She found herself wishing the morning never had to end. The waitress didn't hurry them, bringing pot after pot of hot tea and smiling indulgently at the pair who she probably took for lovers.

Talk turned eventually to her experience so far at Club de Sade. "So how's it going, Ms. Dominatrix? Are you having fun?"

"I am, actually. I still don't really know what I'm doing, but I sure hit the ground running!" She explained about Mistress Jolene's unexpected absence and her being asked to take her client load for the day. "I find I'm kind of touched by the neediness of these submissive guys. I thought at first I would just be catering to freaks and perverts, and maybe they are, but that's not all they are. I mean, there's a real need there, something primal, I think it takes real courage to admit."

Jesse looked appraisingly at her. "You relate, don't you? You understand the submissive psyche in a way you weren't expecting, am I right?"

Carly flushed and looked down. She felt his touch as he lifted her chin with his finger. His voice was low and sexy. "I think there's something there you might want to explore. Something in yourself you haven't really experienced yet."

Carly swallowed. She felt something electric flying between them, not quite articulated but very real. Her stomach was in knots suddenly—he was treading too close to feelings she was just becoming aware she had. Trying to be flip, she pulled her head back a little so he dropped his hand and said in a bantering tone, "Oh, and you're just the man to show me, right?"

Jesse sat back, cocking his head at her. He smiled a little half-smile and said gently, "I could be. We'll have to see."

* * * * *

That night found Carly serving as a hostess at the club's monthly play party. Dressed in her black leather and heels, her hair swept back and long earrings dangling, she felt a new kind of confidence. Perhaps she was just playing a part, but she felt the power of her position surge through her, making her carry herself in a confident, almost regal manner.

The men around her responded in kind, addressing her respectfully as "Mistress". The dungeon was crowded with men and women dressed in everything from full leather gear to nothing at all. Several women were bare to the waist, their breasts clamped with nipple clips that made Carly shudder, her own nipples tingling with sympathy. There were men dressed only in cock cages, their hands chained and cuffed in front of them. Carly knew a lot of it was strictly game playing and dress up, but in the dark setting with pulsing music, low lighting and all the bondage and torture paraphernalia, the effect was quite intense.

She was expected to assist with the "slave auction" that evening. Amanda Merritt, the owner of the club, would conduct the bidding and Carly was to bring out each "slave" and display him or her.

She had only just met Amanda, a large effusive woman who laughed easily and seemed to enjoy herself thoroughly. "So you're the gorgeous new Mistress my Anthony has been gushing about," Amanda had said when introduced. Carly had just been leaving after her first hectic day on the job. She was again dressed in jeans and sneakers, the eye makeup now on a used tissue in the bathroom trash.

"What a sweet little angel you are. I can scarcely imagine you as a Domme. More sub material, no?" Amanda had said, touching Carly's cheek in a familiar way, causing her to blush and step back.

Anthony told her afterwards Amanda was gay. "You'll get to meet her S.O. tomorrow night. They live a very intense, 24/7 type D/s relationship. Betty literally worships the ground Amanda walks on. Amanda will probably bring her to the party. She likes to parade her little slave girl around. She's hopelessly, ridiculously in love with Betty, though she tries to act all butch and tough." He laughed, real affection in his tone for his boss. Carly smiled uncertainly but was distracted by his next remark. "Oh, and Amanda says you'll be doing the auction with her. Good way to give you exposure without you having to do much."

So now Carly stood to the side of the stage. The slaves who were participating were standing together in a nervous bunch. Each one had a cardboard sign over their neck, dangling from a piece of rope. Each sign was painted with a number. Carly was given a silver dog leash. She was to attach it to each slave when they were called and to lead them to the stage by it. Each slave wore a collar of one sort or another.

"It's all just for show. We aren't *really* auctioning slaves, obviously! Not for keeps, anyway. But we give out these chips—" Anthony showed Carly a handful of little red and blue poker chips "—and people can bid on the slaves. Highest bidder gets a 'scene' with the slave, if they so desire and if the slave's master approves, of course. Mainly it's an icebreaker—gets the crowd mingling. People love it. Our auction parties are by far the best attended."

The music was turned down and the lights over the stage were turned on. "Good evening, ladies and gentlemen, Masters and slaves, perverts all." There was laughter as Amanda continued. "Tonight we will auction off the best New York City has to offer. Remember, you can bid as often as you want, but only for the chips you have in your possession. And when you win someone, you need to meet with their owner to coordinate any playing.

"This evening I have a lovely new assistant." She waved toward Carly who felt a sudden surge of adrenaline prickle through her as all eyes turned toward her. "May I present Mistress Marlena. Some of you have had the pleasure of meeting her already, and perhaps have experienced the sting of her whip or the point of her boot." A whoop went up from the audience and Carly saw Tommy, her very first client, grinning widely at her. She smiled back, a little flicker of confidence igniting inside her.

"Number one, come forward," Amanda said in a deep voice. As she had been previously instructed, Carly clipped the leash to the first slave's collar. The room quieted as Carly led her onto the stage, tugging gently at the leash. The first slave was a tall woman with blazing red hair, dressed in a very low-cut black evening gown. Around her neck was a thick black collar. The word "cunt" had been written in large black marker across her breasts. This word, probably handwritten by her "master" took Carly aback. It was so degrading! Yet the woman seemed perfectly calm and happy as she stood next to Carly, waiting for the bidding to begin.

Because the woman was attractive, the bidding was fast and furious, with people quickly using up their chips and trying to borrow chips from their neighbors. She was "sold" to a short, dark man in a white linen suit who looked thoroughly pleased with himself.

Carly removed the leash so she could attach it to the next slave. Amanda said, "Slave number two. Front and center." This slave was male, middle-aged with thinning hair. He was quite tall and thin, still finely muscled, though a little stooped. He was very scantily clad in a little leather loincloth, which reminded Carly of something a Native American might have worn in an old Western. Amanda had to work the crowd a little harder to get the bidding going.

"Mistress Marlena," she said. "Lift that worthless slave's loincloth and let's see what he's made of." Carly didn't react immediately. Was she really saying to expose the man completely? Amanda tapped her foot and made a face at Carly, making a lifting motion with her hand.

Carly obeyed, wondering if the man was dying of embarrassment, but he seemed to be having a grand time. He grinned proudly as Carly lifted the little leather square to reveal a cock and balls completely shaved and pierced with a number of golden rings. Before the eyes of the crowd, his penis lifted like it was being inflated with a bicycle pump until it was fully erect.

Carly stepped back, impressed in spite herself at the size of the man's erect penis. The bidding took off at that point, with the highest bidder being his own mistress, a short, plump woman dressed in an elaborate yellow silk gown, which made her look to Carly like a round yellow beach ball.

She stepped onto the stage before Carly had a chance to escort her charge down. To the delight of the audience the woman took her slave from the stage by grasping his erect cock and leading him none too gently down the steps. "Showoff," Carly heard her mutter, but she was smiling. Carly noticed they wore matching wedding rings.

Eight more slaves were auctioned and as Carly moved up and down the stage stairs she found herself wishing her heels weren't quite so high. Dutifully she led each new slave to the stage and presented them when asked by Amanda—lifting a skirt, exposing a breast or ass.

She couldn't believe she not only had the nerve to treat these subs like this, but she was actually having fun. Of course, it was clear they were having fun, too. When the last slave had been auctioned, the music was turned back up and people began to "scene". This involved slaves being bound to the whipping post or chained to various chairs or tables for their "punishments". They were whipped and teased, fondled and touched. None of it was dangerous and no one was hurt, though some bottoms definitely were reddened and the sting of the lash and crop was real.

"Having fun, Mistress?"

Carly jumped a little. The voice had sounded familiar and for a second she had thought—but no. It was only a client. Not even hers, but someone she had seen in the parlor when she was passing through.

She was polite but non-responsive when he tried to flirt with her. His voice had the timbre of Jesse's but as he spoke she realized the similarities stopped there. This man, who introduced himself as Ben, spent the next fifteen minutes trying to convince her to leave with him, so she could "Dom him good and proper back at his place".

His promises to lick her boots, to be her toilet, to sleep in a cage at her feet did not arouse her in the least, but actually repelled her. Did people really do this stuff? She knew she had to stop being so naïve and get with the program. As far as Ben knew, she was what she presented at this party—Mistress Marlena, dressed in leather, carrying a riding crop, ready to wield it and exercise her dominant impulses on this guy's submissive butt.

Politely she excused herself, going in search of Anthony. She found him near the stage talking with a small woman in her mid-forties dressed in a sheer black robe that revealed her lithe, naked form beneath it. Anthony was wearing a cream-colored silk suit, beautifully tailored, his smooth, tan chest exposed. Carly was startled to realize there was another man kneeling quietly at Anthony's feet. He was dressed in black pants and wore no shirt on his well-muscled torso.

"Ah, Mistress Marlena," Anthony said, turning and smiling. "You were marvelous on stage. A real natural. Stole the show from half those slave wannabes." He turned back toward the woman he was standing with and said, "This is Betty. Amanda's beloved." As Betty blushed prettily, ducking her head, Anthony added, "And this—" he touched the blond head of the man kneeling at his side " —is Jerry. He's my boy toy."

Jerry looked up at Carly and said, "Pleased to meet you, ma'am," as if it was perfectly normal to be kneeling shirtless at another man's feet. At this party, she supposed, it was. They were all distracted when a lovely young woman was led to the whipping post near where they were standing.

She was ordered to strip by her master. A small crowd gathered as she dropped her blouse and slid out of her miniskirt, revealing her naked body beneath. As she was bound to the post, Carly saw she sported a large tattoo of a snake, curling down her back, its tongue darting out just above the crack of her ass.

The man with her took a long, heavy flogger from his bag and drew the tresses down her back. The woman sighed a little but otherwise was still. Slowly he drew back his arm and let the whip fall against her. Carly started a little as leather made contact with flesh, remembering the last time she'd watched such a demonstration.

The man caressed the young woman's skin with his hand for a moment, smoothing the spot he had just struck. He let the lash fall again, harder this time. Soon he worked into a rhythm, systematically covering all the flesh of her back, ass and thighs.

As her skin began to redden, the woman began to moan, pressing erotically against the smooth wood of the post as if it was a lover. Carly watched fascinated as the man's lash seemed to excite the woman into a sexual frenzy. She was moaning loudly now, thrusting and arching her hips as her crotch ground against the post.

Her breath came in little staccato cries as he whipped her in earnest, his strokes matching her erotic dance. When at last he stopped, it was only because she had, sagging in her bonds, her body covered in sweat, her face a study in post-orgasmic bliss.

When Carly fell asleep that night, it was that image, which was imprinted on her brain. She saw the woman's expression, part lust, part agony, part rapture, and she found her fingers slipping down to her own needy pussy, though she only dimly understood the impulses that drove her.

Chapter Six

ജ

Carly began to settle into a routine at the club. She'd successfully passed her "probationary" period of two weeks and had received her own key. She had a slowly growing roster of her own clients as well as the "walk-ins" she was expected to handle. Carly, or Mistress Marlena as she was known at Club de Sade, was beginning to build a reputation for herself. If her clients were at first fooled by her innocent good looks and small stature, they soon realized she was a force to be reckoned with.

As she became more comfortable in her new role as Dominatrix, Carly found herself actually thrilling to the power and control aspects of her job. Yet at the same time she didn't want to abuse the trust these men handed her. She actually found herself keenly identifying with their submissive urges and longings in a way that surprised her.

She would flinch along with her sub when she stroked them with a whip or welted their bare skin with a cane. She was careful—probably too careful at first. She didn't want to truly hurt her charges or break the skin. They actually guided her with their responses and even made suggestions when the heat of the moment had passed. She took her job seriously, applying herself as she had in any other job, putting her whole self into it. The image of the lovely young woman at her first play party had stayed in the back of her mind, beckoning silently though she couldn't hear the words.

She found herself wondering what it would feel like to be on the receiving end of such treatment. She found herself admiring the true grace with which some of her clients submitted—handling a whipping with barely a tremor, their eyes closed, their faces reflecting something like rapture.

Perhaps it was precisely this strong identification with her charges that made Carly such a good Dominatrix. She understood on some kind of visceral level what moved and motivated them and she identified, perhaps too strongly, she sometimes thought.

She'd begun to read about the submissive psyche, at first telling herself it was strictly for research purposes. Obviously she needed to understand the sort of person she was dealing with so she could effectively control and arouse them. Perhaps it went beyond that, though how far beyond she wasn't yet sure.

She had purchased several books on the subject, including some novels that looked kind of sexy. As she read, the books gave her food for thought. What would it be like to be in love with a dominant man? To be his "slave" as well as his lover? As always these days when she thought of romance, her thoughts drifted to Jesse. They'd gone out twice in the two weeks since their first breakfast, once to dinner and a movie and once to a dance club. He'd kissed her at the end of each date, a long, lingering kiss that made her breath quicken and her pussy moisten, but it hadn't moved beyond that.

Carly was used to men pushing themselves on her — eager to come up to her apartment after the first date. She had told Jesse most men she had known were too forward and expected too much too soon from a woman. Now she almost regretted sharing that information. The one time she would like a man to move forward, he seemed to be hanging back! Though she behaved in an outgoing manner, Carly was basically shy when it came to men. She found she didn't have the nerve to try and move the situation along.

It was six-thirty on a Wednesday evening at the end of October. The clouds looked fat and gray, portending rain or maybe even snow. Carly had no clients scheduled and Anthony had told her they had enough staff that evening to handle any walk-ins. Carly was snuggled up in her bed with a good book, happy for a quiet evening. She'd been working pretty steadily since she'd started at Club de Sade. With the first week's pay, she'd purchased several more sexy outfits and a few little whips that had caught her eye at a BDSM boutique in the Village. At the rate things were going, soon she would be able to pay off her credit cards and maybe even start saving some money for the first time in her life.

The phone rang and Carly jumped. She knew Jesse was out of town again, pursuing some "lead" in one of his cases. Eva and George had a date. Who could be calling?

"Hello?"

"Oh, good. Glad I caught you! Listen, Carly," it was Anthony, his voice breathless, urgent. "Jolene's bailed on us! Flew the coop! She called from Indiana, for crying out loud! Apparently she's in some kind of trouble and she's gone to hide out at her mom's. Anyway, long story short, she has a couple of clients scheduled for tonight and if there's any way I can do it, I want them covered. Looks bad for the club when we stand up the clients. I have her seven o'clock taken care of but I was wondering, hoping, *praying*, that you, Mistress Marlena, could take her eight o'clock. Please, oh, please, say you will. I'm sure I can convince Amanda to pay you a little extra for the inconvenience."

So much for a quiet night at home. She glanced out the little window. It dark and cold, and she didn't relish the idea of waiting for the bus in that weather. If she walked an extra three blocks she could take the subway, she supposed. Sighing just a little she said, "I'll be there."

The subway trip had taken longer than Carly had expected because a train had somehow stalled on the tracks, preventing her train from arriving for a full twenty minutes. Now she barely had time to pull on her outfit and read the client folder—it was seven forty-five.

Anthony looked at his watch and pursed his lips a little as Carly explained about the subway mishap. "Well, I *forgive* you," he said, annoying her a little—she felt frazzled enough. "I'll send him up when he gets here—" again he consulted his watch "—in ten minutes! Here's the client data. Scoot on up to the blue room and transform yourself, Mistress."

As she took the client data folder he added, "Oh, you'll see it in the folder, but just so you're ready, this one's a knife player. He's on the edge of the kink, the darker edge. Be careful with him because he'll go as far as you take him and press for more."

Now he tells me, Carly thought. Up until that point, she'd been given the "easy" ones—light bondage, a little whipping. Would she be up to this "darker" client? Anthony still labored under the illusion she was experienced and she wasn't about to disabuse him of that notion now. Clutching the little folder and her trusty duffel, Carly hurried up to the blue room.

With her short hair slicked back with gel, makeup applied and dressed in a dark crimson corset over burgundy leather pants, Mistress Marlena crossed her legs, dangling one stiletto-heeled foot over her knee, trying to catch her breath from her quick change act.

Flipping open the folder she read. *Hank. Likes—verbal humiliation, tight bondage, total nudity, intense knife play, especially at the throat. Dislikes—gentle treatment, praise. Likes it very rough.*

"I can do this," she told herself, taking a deep breath. When the knock came, Carly jumped up and stumbled a little on her heels. "Steady, girl," she muttered and then louder, "Come in."

"Mistress Marlena, I've brought some scum for you to train. His own mistress is too disgusted to have anything more to do with him. She's giving him to you because of your reputation with knives and your passion for spilling a man's blood."

Carly saw the little man standing behind Anthony, his head bowed. He was dressed in a rumpled brown suit and white shirt with a striped tie. A jolt of familiarity ripped through Carly before she could process it. As he lifted his balding head to look at her, time, which had been going along normally up to that point, seemed to stop, to freeze into slow motion like some horrible nightmare. Carly barely heard Anthony's little speech about her supposed abilities. All she could do was stare.

Of all the BDSM clubs in all towns in all the world, why had *he* stumbled into hers? There before her stood her hated ex-boss Henry R. Franklin. And *she* was expected to be his Dominatrix for the next hour. Carly stood poised between hysterical laughter and a shrill squeal. Anthony looked at her, concern evident in his face.

"You okay?" he mouthed.

Slowly she nodded. She'd let Franklin make the call. She was here, dressed and ready to earn a little extra cash. *Hey*, she thought, her practical nature rising to the fore, *why not make some money and extract some kind of cosmic revenge in the process*? Her ex-boss was going to die when he saw who his new mistress was.

As Henry Franklin lifted his head there was a little smile on his weak-chinned face. The smile froze, cracked and slid off his features as he took in his ex-employee Carly Stevens aka Mistress Marlena.

True, she looked quite different with her heavy makeup and sexy, tight clothing, which emphasized her bosom and shapely legs. Yet she saw the recognition dawn on his face as he paled and turned to Anthony.

"I-I can't," he spluttered, seeming to have a difficulty articulating his thoughts. "A mistake," he managed.

"No mistake, slave boy." Anthony's voice was hard, a lower register than his usual effeminate singsong. Carly had a glimpse of what he might be like when he was playing Dom. "You've been brought to the best knife handler in the business. She'll make you piss on yourself with fear—she's that good. You're going strip off your clothes like a good little sub boy and then you're going to sit yourself down, let yourself be tied to that chair and experience some of the most intense knife play you can get in a club."

"But you don't understand," Henry tried again. Anthony ignored him, assuming perhaps his protests were part of the game. He pushed the much shorter man toward the chair and barked, "Strip, boy! You belong to us now. You have no choice in the matter. Move!"

Henry turned toward Carly, his eyes bugging, his mouth working. Yet somehow his trembling fingers were unbuttoning his shirt, loosening his tie, pulling down his pants. The man was going to do it! He clearly recognized Carly just as she had recognized him, but he was taking off his clothing as Anthony had commanded!

"I'll leave you to your torture," Anthony said as he flipped the little timer on the night table. Again he looked curiously at Carly, a question in his face.

"I'm all right," she mouthed silently. Satisfied, he left the room, closing the door quietly behind him. Turning toward Henry, Carly saw he had stripped down to his boxers. He stood uncertainly, twisting his hands in front of him. She couldn't help but notice the erection in his underwear. Whatever he must be feeling, a part of him was turned on.

She decided to play her role to the hilt, and hopefully have some fun in the process. If only she could tell Eva about this! "Boy," she said, her voice low, "are you ready to suffer for me?"

"Stevens, this is most irregular—"

She cut him off sharply. "How *dare* you, slave! You are to address me by my proper title—Mistress Marlena. Go ahead. Get on your knees and apologize properly!"

She waited the fraction of a second it took to see what he would do. This would define their interactions going forward, she knew. To her delight, the little man dropped awkwardly to his knees. "I-I apologize, Mistress. Mistress Marlena. I had you confused with someone."

"Did you." Her tone was sardonic. "Well, don't let it happen again, slave. For that you'll need to be doubly punished. Get up! Pull down those ridiculous boxers and show me your pathetic little package!"

Carly felt at once horrified and amused as her domineering ex-boss blushed and fumbled with his underpants, pulling them down and off. Ridiculously he stood naked except for his black socks. His cock was fully erect and larger than Carly would have expected, given his short stature.

"Sit," she commanded imperiously. As he complied, settling himself in the torture chair, Carly selected a knife with a long, thin blade. She swallowed her own nervousness — this was definitely a strange position in which to find herself! Part of her wanted to slit the bastard's throat for the living hell he'd made her life when she'd worked for him. But another part acknowledged her obligations to her new alter ego. Mistress Marlena wouldn't let personal feelings get in the way of using her client properly.

Whatever else Henry Franklin was, at the moment he was a client of Club de Sade who had a right to expect his mistress to provide the services for which he would pay handsomely.

Carly moved to secure the man's legs and wrists into the waiting leather straps. She turned the handle to spread his legs, leaving his still-erect cock and balls jutting out lewdly. Henry was breathing shallowly and fast, almost as if he was already near orgasm. *What must he be feeling*, she wondered? At the mercy of someone he knew had a right to hate him! A masochist's dream? Well, she planned to make his dreams come true, at least for an hour.

It was hard to reconcile this groveling little man who sat bound and naked before her with the man who had spent the last year systematically destroying her credibility and career at the catalog company, stealing her ideas, sabotaging her efforts and taking the credit for her successes.

As she stood tall in her heels, a long, thin knife in her hand, her ex-boss immobilized in front of her, Carly gave in for a moment to petty feelings of revenge. She slapped his jowly cheek with her open palm. Henry's eyes widened but as his cheek reddened he murmured, "Thank you, Mistress."

Carly felt a thrill of power. What a strange situation! She shifted fully into "Mistress Marlena" mode as she regarded her client. "How does it feel to be naked, bound and at my mercy? Are you prepared to suffer?"

"Yes, Mistress," Henry whispered, his cock bobbing. Carly slapped it hard and knelt down so her face was level with his. Slowly she brought the tip of the knife to Henry's throat.

"You like it rough, huh, slave? You'd like me to press this knife just a little harder, wouldn't you, you filth? Press the point so a bright red drop of blood rolls down your neck. I'd do it in a flash, boy, if the law allowed. I'd cut you and then smear the blood on your lips. Make you lick it up. You'd like that, wouldn't you, you pathetic little slave?" One part of Carly couldn't believe she was talking this way. But then, it wasn't Carly, it was Mistress Marlena, wasn't it?

"Yes, ma'am, oh, yes!" Henry was panting now, obviously deeply aroused by her treatment and her words. Carly drew the knife carefully down the side of his neck, the point grazing his shoulder, his nipple, his breastbone. She drew it past his paunch, leaving a pink mark as the point scraped his skin. When she touched his cock with the blade Henry jerked forward so the point poked him rather harder than she had intended.

A tiny drop of blood appeared on the tip of his penis and Carly panicked a moment. This was definitely not allowed and she certainly hadn't intended to really hurt him! But Henry went wild, bucking and arching against his cuffs.

"Oh, God! Mistress, please! I need this." His voice was raised, almost a shout. "You are so incredibly sexy! Thank you, Mistress. Do it again. Make me bleed! I am slime. I am filth. You are so hot! Do it! Cut me! Cut me! Please!"

Carly stood back now thoroughly shaken up. He was so loud—so demanding! Just like back in the office, though now it was surreal and too bizarre for words. Grabbing his boxers Carly rushed toward the bound man and shouted, "Open your mouth, slave. I'm tired of your noise!" Her voice was commanding and he did as he was told. She quickly wadded and pressed the fabric into his mouth.

Feeling more in control now Carly said, "That was a little treat. Don't expect it to happen again. You don't deserve it. Now I'm going to punish you for your demands. You seem to forget *I* am the Mistress here—you are the slave."

Henry nodded, his slightly protruding eyes bugging out at her with evident adoration. She dabbed at the head of his cock with a tissue to get the bit of blood she'd inadvertently drawn. Luckily it was only a tiny puncture and had stopped bleeding of its own accord.

Carly took a set of clothespins and began attaching them to Henry's balls. He grunted with each pinch but his cock remained as hard as steel—a silent indication he approved of the proceedings.

When she was done, having attached six pins, she stood back and said, "Does it hurt, slave?"

As Henry nodded she answered, "Good." Again she took the knife, drawing it carefully up and down his body as she whispered about the tortures she would inflict upon him when she had him in her chambers, creating a fantasy for him which included kidnapping him and cutting him with various knives until he was covered in blood.

A part of her was horrified with her own descriptions. She was aware she was going beyond any pretend cruelty she had yet practiced with her masochistic clients. She knew on one level a real rage fueled some of her comments and she also knew this could be potentially dangerous behavior on her part.

Yet no matter how outrageous her remarks, Henry only seemed to stiffen further with arousal, panting behind his cotton gag so hard his whole body was heaving. "You want to come, don't you, you sick fuck?" Carly hissed, her voice low and hard as nails.

Henry nodded wildly and as her fingers grazed his arms, coming up to circle his throat he bucked and ejaculated, a clot of semen landing on her leather-clad leg. Carly stood back, nonplussed. She had planned to release his wrists and let him jerk himself off. His premature ejaculation had caught her off-guard.

Recovering she said, "Oh, Hanky boy, you really blew it this time." She smiled a cruel little smile. "I didn't give you *permission* to come. I only asked you if you wanted to. Now you're going to have to pay for that. Aren't you?"

Eagerly he bobbed his head, breathing hard through his nostrils, the damp underwear still held in his teeth.

Carly unbuckled his wrists and ankles and said, "Go on, lick off that nasty come, you slime. Clean my leg, little doggie."

Henry dropped to all fours, the clothespins still pinching his scrotum. Obediently he knelt up and licked at her leg. Carly resisted her impulse to push him down, to kick him. After all, she was the one who told him to do this. Again the surreal nature of this bizarre hour washed over her.

After he'd licked off the little pearly blobs of ejaculate, Carly pushed him away and said, "Crawl like the dog you are." Henry crawled around the room, his penis again rising to half-mast. She let him go for a minute or so and then said, "Stand up."

Henry stood in front of her. With her four-inch heels, she stood slightly taller than he. Standing very close to him, she reached down and removed the clothespins. With each released spring, Henry hissed his pained appreciation as the tortured nerve endings pulsed back to life.

Impulsively he knelt and began to kiss Carly's feet, licking the soft leather of her high heels with his broad, flat tongue. Between licks he murmured, "Thank you, Mistress, thank you, Mistress. Thank you! Please don't send me back to Mistress Jolene. I belong to you! I was born for you! Please, I adore you."

Carly pulled back, not quite taking it in yet. As she processed what he was saying she realized her hated ex-boss was begging her to make him her permanent client. What a peculiar turn the evening was taking.

The hour over, Henry pulled on his clothing, jumping from foot to foot as he pulled up his trousers. He kept glancing at his watch, his expression worried. She allowed him to dress without interference and silently accepted the hundred-dollar tip he thrust her way. He hurried to the door, turning back to say, "Thank you again, Mistress Marlena. You were sublime. Please accept me as your humble slave."

Though she didn't say she would take him as a permanent client, she didn't say she wouldn't.

* * * * *

Mrs. Franklin pursed her lips, crossed her arms over her bony chest and tapped her foot impatiently. Henry was late again. She spied him as he turned the corner of her block, striding quickly toward her. As he approached, she glanced pointedly at her watch.

His jacket looked rumpled and what wisps of hair he had left were askew. The man was impossible. How could you become so disheveled from attending a Rotary meeting? Every Wednesday evening for the past six months Henry had escorted his wife to her bible study meeting at the Metropolitan Tabernacle Church before going on the two blocks west and one block north to the Rotary Club where he claimed to be developing business contacts and "doing good" for the community. He was rather vague about it all, but Mrs. Franklin certainly approved of good works.

She'd given up trying to get him to attend her church meetings. The few times she had managed to drag him, he'd snored so loudly she had been thoroughly embarrassed. The man was going to hell. Why she'd ever let him talk her into marrying him she didn't know.

Well, if she was honest, she did know. At thirty-three, she wasn't getting any younger and so far no proposals had come her way. Not that she sought them out, no sir. Since she had been a young woman she had had the calling, just like her mother. Jesus needed her to do his good work on earth, converting those worth saving and condemning those who were bound for hell. She never hesitated to let the young men who came around know just where she stood on issues of good and evil. They didn't usually come around a second time, but that was their loss as her mother assured her.

When Henry Franklin, a mere bookkeeper at her father's catalog company, had shyly asked her at a company picnic if she would care for some more potato salad, she had taken notice. Thirty-eight at the time, he had never married. She should have been more suspicious because of that but back then she was a trusting, simple girl. He had seemed a nice enough fellow, before he became too big for his britches with the steady promotions he was given at her father's company.

Edna knew it was not his merit, but her father's desire to see she lived in comfort and security that prompted him to continue to promote his lackluster son-in-law. Everything Henry R. Franklin was he owed to Edna and her father, and she never let him forget it.

When Edna had wanted to move back to New York last year—Chicago was too windy and dreary—her father had found a position for Henry, just like he always did and they'd moved in due course. She'd promptly found a church that suited her tastes. Reverend Johnson was an excellent speaker and didn't skirt around the serious issues like hellfire and damnation as so many of these mealy-mouthed preachers did these days. She did so admire his striking good looks—his silver hair brushed straight back from a high forehead, his prominent features and blazing eyes. He was tall and handsome—everything Henry was not. And he wasn't afraid to speak the truth.

The Reverend's sermon tonight had been particularly inspiring, detailing the ravages of eternal hell that awaited the sinners who filled this huge city, teaming like maggots in its belly. Edna received an almost sexual charge from this sort of sermon, though she wouldn't have recognized it as such and certainly wouldn't have admitted it.

She pulled her coat more snugly around herself as Henry came trotting and puffing up to her. "You're late," she informed him acidly. "I'm freezing."

"So sorry, dear. I was detained. An accountant from Barkley's was bending my ear."

"Save your excuses. You look like a mess. What have you been doing? You look more like you've been in a fight than at a Rotary meeting." She peered down her nose at him as he ducked his head, looking guilty as usual.

As they walked the six blocks home — Edna didn't approve of public transportation and saw no point in taking taxis when their legs worked just fine — she told Henry about the sermon. Her eyes began to shine as she expostulated on Reverend Johnson's themes of eternal punishment for the sinners here on earth.

"This city's full of sinners, Henry. Nasty, dirty sinners who take the Lord's name in vain, who profane his image with their filthy sex and crimes against nature. It makes me sick. Sick, I tell you."

Henry nodded, barely seeming to listen. Edna lapsed into silence after a while. The man was hopeless. She was convinced he was on his way to hell with the rest of them, and good riddance. In the afterlife she would sit on the right hand of God while he writhed in the burning fires below.

Edna touched her stomach unconsciously. How she hated Henry and yet the primary reason she hated him wasn't his fault or at least it was beyond his control. He had never given her a child. Edna was already in her thirties when they married, that was true, but she wasn't barren. The doctor had assured her she was in good working order. Dutifully each Friday night she let Henry climb on her, rutting and panting like some kind of sweaty, stinking animal until he shot his seed into her womb. She knew it was her Christian duty to accept this behavior and she knew it was the only way to make a baby. A child she could mold and shape in her own image, honest and God-fearing.

Yet the months and then the years had passed and still God didn't grace them with a child. Edna became increasingly embittered and now it was too late. Eventually Henry had stopped touching her altogether and though on the one hand she was just as glad, on the other her feelings were hurt. It was clear he had no interest in her, except for the easy living his job provided them, and the fine home her father bought for them in Chicago, and later the condominium in New York.

The more Henry turned from her, the more she turned toward the church, finding solace and succor in the fiery bosom of the angry God she chose to embrace. Revenge against evildoers was one of her favorite themes. Secretly she wanted revenge against Henry, though she would have denied this, even to herself.

She wouldn't divorce him—she believed in her vows, including "until death do us part". And though she caught him in the occasional affair, she hadn't done much about it, except berate and admonish him to change his evil ways. Each betrayal on his part just pushed them further apart.

Now they mostly lived parallel lives, eating dinner together and sharing a bedroom, though they had twin beds since he snored and she couldn't abide that phlegmy rumble in her ear.

The Rotary Club had been his idea, an attempt to network in the city, he had told her. It made sense to her and she had approved. She was very loyal to her father's company and, as his only child, expected to inherit it one day. Since her seven-thirty Wednesday night church meeting was on the way to Henry's eight o'clock meeting, she had him escort her there and go on to his meeting.

"What do you do at those meetings?" she asked suddenly. Henry who had been walking quietly beside her, lost in thought, jumped a little.

"Eh? What meetings?"

"The Rotary Club meetings, you fool. What else?"

"Oh, that. We, uh, read the minutes from the last meeting. We do good works. We make contacts, you know. Good leads for the L. J. Smathers & Co. Very important leads, very important contacts. All for the business, all for your father's business."

Edna glanced sidelong at her husband. She could tell he was lying—she always knew. But she didn't know what he was lying about. Why lie about what the Rotary Club did? What was he up to?

She kept her counsel. He would never admit he was lying and if he suspected she thought he was, he'd get crafty. He was a sneaky little bastard. She had caught him twice in lies about other women back in Chicago. He could stick his nasty little thing in someone else for all she cared. She certainly had no interest in it. Still, the insult of his implied rejection of her pricked and rankled as it always did, exacerbating the secret, festering pain in her heart.

That night as Edna was drifting off to sleep, a much-read bible still clenched in her hand, Henry who had fallen asleep perhaps a half hour before in his own bed, shifted and muttered. Edna sat up, leaning toward him to hear what he was saying. He quieted though and she lay back down.

A moment later however he moaned, a long, low sound and said quite distinctly, "Thank you, Mistress," before subsiding back to a rumbly snore.

Chapter Seven

ഔ

The candlelight was romantic, the food was delicious and the wine was making her a little giddy. Jesse leaned over the little table at the Cuban restaurant he had invited Carly to and said, "I think I may be falling in love."

Carly colored a little, a dimple appearing in her right cheek. She wanted to say, "me too", but the words didn't quite come out. Instead she said, "I'm having a lovely evening, Jesse. The food, the company — it's all perfect."

Jesse smiled. "Okay, I'll take that." He took a drink of his wine and asked, "So, how's it going at the club? Is the bloom still on the rose?"

It was the Friday after Carly's fateful meeting with Hank aka Henry Franklin. Though Carly was dying to confide the strange tale to Jesse, she knew she mustn't break confidence. Instead she kept her remarks neutral.

"Things are actually going very well. I didn't realize I had such a knack for domination," she grinned. "The men seem to be falling all over themselves to be my subs! I have a full client list already! I can work as many hours as I can stand to be crammed into my bustier and boots!" She laughed and Jesse laughed with her.

He said, "Well, it's hard work, there's no doubt about that! It's not like with a lover where the passion and joy make it sheer pleasure. No offense intended here and I'm sure you *are* a skilled Dominatrix, but just your good looks alone would ensure the men are falling all over themselves to be with you."

She beamed at him but said, "Oh, come on. I mean, thanks for the compliment and all, but give me more credit. I agree, guys might be willing to shell out the bucks the first time for a pretty face—" she smile self-deprecatingly "—but would they keep coming back? Might as well just go to a hooker if that's all you want, no?"

"You're right and I apologize. I was being flippant. So tell me—" Jesse relaxed back into his chair "—why do you think you're so good? Do you get aroused Domming them? Does it turn you on to tie them up and make them obey you?"

Maybe it was the wine, maybe it was because she was beginning to feel very comfortable with Jesse as a friend— though things still hadn't gone any further than a kiss—maybe it was a combination of the two, but Carly found herself answering more openly than she had meant to.

"Oh, no, it isn't that. It's that I identify with them. I understand them."

"You *are* them," Jesse offered softly, his hand slipping over hers on the table.

Their eyes met and though she felt the heat in her face, Carly didn't look away. "Yes," she whispered.

* * * * *

Carly stood in Jesse's apartment in a high-rise building complete with doorman—very impressive. His place was on the twentieth floor, with a stunning view of the Hudson River. She looked around, admiring the sparse Scandinavian furniture in rich blond woods and soft leathers. "Wow, this is some place, Jesse. I didn't realize being a private investigator could earn you so much money! Or is it your BDSM seminars that make all this possible?" She waved her arm around the living room, which, while certainly not huge, was as big as her entire efficiency apartment. For a Manhattan apartment, it was quite comfortable indeed.

Jesse laughed and said, "Unfortunately neither one is that lucrative, though I do okay. But I was lucky with this place. It's rent-controlled and I was able to take the lease over from a cousin of mine who lived here for twenty years before the area became trendy, when it was just a bunch of warehouses and run-down apartment buildings."

A large framed photograph over the living room couch caught Carly's eye. Moving closer she murmured, "That's quite an image."

"Oh, do you like it? That's Amy. She loved being tied up."

"This is amazing." The photo had been blown up to poster size and framed in silver. It was black and white, which somehow made it more arresting. A tall, young woman was tethered between two trees, only their trunks visible. Her arms were stretched high above her head, each one secured to low hanging branches on either side of her. Her legs were similarly spread so she formed a large X between the trunks. Thick rope wrapped her otherwise naked body, covering all of her except her breasts, which were bare, the nipples erect. Her head was dropped back so her face was obscured, long pale hair streaming behind her. If that image wasn't striking enough, it was the angle of the setting sun that made it truly a work of art. The rays literally lit her up from behind so she seemed to glow like some fallen angel captured here on earth.

"You took this?" Carly's admiration was clear in her voice.

"Yeah. Usually I forget to put film in a camera or I leave the flash on when it shouldn't be or vice versa. Purely a fluke it came out like that. I liked the image so I had it blown up."

"She's gorgeous," Carly added, hoping the jealously she suddenly felt wasn't showing in her voice. Was this Amy still in the picture?

As if reading her mind Jesse offered, "I haven't seen Amy in maybe three years. I thought for a while she was the one, but things didn't work out. Guess I've been looking ever since for my dream submissive. I wonder if I've found her?"

Carly didn't answer. The usual niggling doubt sounded in the back of her brain—if they made love, and she was pretty sure that was where things were headed at last, it would be all over. The connection they felt would dwindle like so much ash after the fire, blown by the winds of misplaced desire. Sex ruined everything, or it had in the past. Scales would fall from her eyes and the man who had seemed so desirable would become someone she couldn't wait to get away from. Eva had told her this was very "masculine" of her—a typical male reaction—once you get the girl, you don't want her anymore. Carly wasn't sure of the dynamic, but she knew it left her lonely and sad and a little less open the next time to intimacy.

Yet this felt different. It had to be. The warmth when his hand grazed hers started deep in her belly, moving through her veins like something vital and powerful and good. She hushed her own demons—she wanted this man.

They stood together looking out his window at the barges twinkling on the river. When he leaned down to her, she lifted her face, her eyes closed, her lips tingling. His kiss was warm and tender at first, but its passion soon heated them both. His hands came up to cradle her head, grasping her hair as he kissed her more ardently, his mouth hot against hers. She responded with parted lips, her tongue slipping into his mouth.

Carly felt her body come alive. The usual seeds of doubts and hesitation when she was first intimate with a man didn't seem to be there. The usual mismatch, however slight—the way a new lover kissed, his scent, his overeagerness or studied casualness—just simply wasn't there. Instead something tiny but insistent inside her was whispering as loud as it could over the roiling blood of her sexual arousal—*he's the one, he's the one.*

It was Jesse who pulled away first. When she didn't feel his lips upon hers, she opened her eyes. Jesse was staring down at her, his expression difficult to read.

She suddenly felt embarrassed and a little confused. What was going on? Answering her unspoken question Jesse said, "I want you. But on my terms. I'm not willing to settle for a casual toss in the sheets with you, Carly. I think we can have so much more. I want to take my time with you. I want to help you explore your submissive feelings."

Carly felt her stomach grip. She wasn't ready to analyze just why. "Jesse, I'm not submissive. I think you may have misunderstood me earlier. I just connect with these guys because I can relate somehow. I mean, I don't know. I might be a little, uh, submissive, but I'm a liberated woman. You know, I stand on my own two feet."

Jesse smiled and lifted a hand to stroke her hair. "Of course you do. Being an independent, freethinking woman and being submissive aren't mutually exclusive. In fact, to be truly submissive you *have* to be sure of yourself. Willing to take risks. Open to new possibilities and brave enough to explore them. Submission is not for the weak or passive, that's for sure."

"Well, I would never put up with the crap those guys want me to do to them. No way!" Carly stuck out her chin defiantly and Jesse laughed again.

"Of course you wouldn't, sweetheart. But what you give your clients has very little to do with submission." He shook his head and amended. "Well, that's not entirely true. I mean, I do believe many of your clients do have submissive feelings. Certainly masochistic ones. But what I want, what I think you might want, is different. Just like sex with a prostitute is different from romantic love. With your boys, it's just game playing. It's business. They pay you to titillate them. You may chain them up and spank their butts, but there's certainly nothing romantic about it."

Jesse took Carly's hand and guided her to the sofa. "What makes you think I want that? Romantic submission? I've never said that. I never fantasized about it. I don't really know how I feel about it."

"I believe you, Carly. I believe you don't know yet. But don't forget, I watched you while you were observing my demonstration with Angela that first night. You weren't just casually interested. You were rapt. Your expression, your demeanor, your body language were eloquent with longing. You have the imprint—something I can't quite define, but I've definitely seen it before. You have the mark of a sub."

Carly stared at him, remembering that night, and how Jake Mitchell had also assumed she was submissive, telling her she had that "certain something" and claiming he was rarely wrong. What did she have, a big red S on her forehead? How could they tell when she herself wasn't even sure?

Though she hadn't been entirely truthful with Jesse. Some residual need to protect herself had kept her from admitting to him she *did* entertain some submissive fantasies, especially since she'd gotten into the scene herself. And those fantasies involved Jesse as her "master". Nothing too intense—no whips or chains, just a strong man taking what he wanted, having his way with her. More along the lines of a romance novel than a S&M story.

"I want to try a little exercise with you. Nothing too serious." Jesse grinned at her and Carly smiled back, dropping her arms. She had, she realized, been holding herself rather protectively.

"The first thing is I want you, just for these next few minutes, to *stop* thinking this all through. Stop analyzing, questioning, worrying."

As she started to respond, to protest, he put a finger against her lips and said, "Oh, and stop talking, too. I just want to try something with you. A little exercise, if you will. It might make things clearer for both of us." Carly looked up at him with her big blue eyes but stayed silent as he had bid.

"Good," he said. "Now, here's what I want you to do. I'm going to kiss you. You are not to respond. Don't touch me, don't kiss me back. Don't move. Just sit there, unless I want you to stand, in which case I'll let you know. You are not to do a thing. Can you do that?"

"Well, I can, but what's the point? I—"

"Shh." Again he touched his finger to her lips. "Don't worry about the point. Trust me just this little bit. I won't do anything you don't want me to do, I promise you."

Carly nodded, puzzled but intrigued. "Okay," Jesse said. "Now we begin. And remember, whatever I do, don't respond, not with words or with your body. Keep as still as you can."

Carly sat on the edge of the couch, uncertain of what was happening. Jesse was the most unusual man she had ever met. He kept her slightly off-balance. Instead of upsetting her though, she found it exciting, even a trifle dangerous—but in a sexy way.

His first kiss was on her eyelid, forcing her to close her eyes. His mouth was warm and soft as he kissed first one then the other eye. Tucking her curls behind her ears, he knelt in front of her and leaned over to kiss her earlobe. It tickled a little and Carly shifted, suppressing a giggle.

"Be still," he whispered, before kissing her other earlobe. Butterfly kisses graced her cheeks, her forehead, her throat. At her neck the light kisses changed and she could feel his tongue glide out, tasting the flesh just over her pulsing artery. His teeth nudged her there, just enough for her to feel their potential. Then his tongue was back, teasing her soft skin and making her shiver.

She started to turn her head, silently willing him to kiss her mouth. "Uh-uh," he admonished. "Don't move. It's the one command I've given you. Can't you obey it? Stay still."

Gently he turned her face forward. She felt chagrined and annoyed. She wanted a kiss! A real kiss like the earlier kiss they'd just shared, tongues intertwined, his hands gripping her hair, melting her insides, she wanted that again, and now!

Instead his tongue found her throat again, sliding along the small bump of her voice box down to the hollow of her collarbone. He slipped lower, his chin grazing her breast.

Her nipples were suddenly violently aware of his presence. She felt them perking and straining against the lace of her bra. Perhaps if she stayed very still he would kiss her breasts next. With casual deliberateness, Jesse unbuttoned the first and then the second buttons of Carly's blouse. She felt her nipples stiffen further, if that was possible.

Carly took a deep, tremulous breath, determined to obey his "one command" if only to show she had some self-discipline. As she drew in the breath, her breasts were raised and extended so the tips were presented to Jesse, though he seemed to be completely unaware of the sweet offering.

Instead he focused on her breastbone, kissing it lightly. Surely he felt her heart, now hammering with need. He smelled so good! She wanted to grab his head and force his lips to hers. Or press it down to find the hard nubbins of her breasts that needed suckling.

As his hot breath teased her skin, she felt his fingers on her blouse again, unbuttoning them all so it fell open. Her eyes flew open and she looked down at his dark shiny hair as he knelt in front of her. Her own skin she saw was mottled with desire, her chest heaving. Still she sat with her hands on either side of her, willing herself to be still. She could do this! She was master of herself.

Surely in a moment he would relent. Wasn't he on fire for her as she was for him? She closed her eyes, dropping her head back. If he wouldn't kiss her mouth, she was sure he would find her breasts, barely covered in feminine lace and satin, too alluring to ignore. She waited for the feel of his hot, perfect mouth against her nipple.

Instead he was kissing her belly, light, sweet kisses, almost chaste. Her skirt still covered her lower half. She found herself wishing at this moment she was naked. Wishing those kisses would extend, lower and lower, as she parted her legs to offer her secret flower for his touch...

In her limited experience, it was always the man in a hurry, eager to "cut to the chase" of intercourse. Foreplay was just that—something that had to be done to "prime" the girl. She had usually felt rushed, or "given in" to get it over with. She had never, she suddenly realized, had a mature sexual relationship. She had never been with a man who understood the power and the pleasure of withholding something until it was all there was.

Her mind shut down again as his mouth finally grazed her nipples, though they were still clad in pink satin and lace. Gently he bit and teased each one until a soft moan of pleasure escaped her lips. Her pussy was so wet she felt a trickle of moisture against her thigh and her panties were soaked.

Carly was a hairsbreadth away from forcing herself on him when Jesse said softly, "Stand up." On shaky legs she stood, almost faint with desire. Slowly he pulled the opened blouse from her body. His face was flushed and his dark eyes were shining with intensity. At least he wasn't impervious — he wanted her, too.

"What are you willing to do for me?"

"Anything," she murmured fervently, before she had time to censor herself. When she realized what she had said, she tried to backtrack. "That is, uh, I mean. I wanted a kiss, that's all."

"Please, Carly. Don't do it. Don't try to control what is natural and beautiful in you. We both know it's there. Let's find the courage to explore it together."

On a primal level she understood him. She knew he was right, though she didn't yet have the full understanding or insight to act upon it. When he reached back to unzip her skirt she didn't protest.

As it fell to a little heap at her feet, she stepped out of it. She was wearing thigh-high stockings that didn't require garters. They matched the pale pink satin of her panties and bra. The effect created was a combination of innocence and wanton sexuality.

She lifted her face to his, eagerly waiting for the kiss she was sure would now be forthcoming — her eyes fluttering shut in blissful anticipation. This time he didn't disappoint her, his mouth taking hers, claiming her, leaving her weak and trembling in his arms.

Again it was Jesse who pulled away. "I want to make love to you, Carly. On my terms. Do you want that?"

"What do you mean?" Carly found she could barely catch her breath. Her mouth was imprinted with his kisses and she was hungry for more. As his fingers slid down her flat belly to rest lightly over the little patch of satin that covered her mons she knew she would agree to any terms, as long as they included this delicious man making love to her.

"I mean you will belong to me, if just for tonight. Suspend your fears, your questions, your anxieties about sex ruining everything—" *how did he know that?* "—and give yourself over to me. Let me take you on a guided submissive journey. Let me just show you the possibilities. No strings, no commitments—just a taste of what things could be."

His fingers slipped inside her panties and she made no move to stop him. She couldn't suppress the little sigh that escaped her lips as he stroked the wet folds of her sex, certainly aware of the effect he was having. "No fair," she managed, though her body betrayed her as she involuntarily arched toward his hand.

"It won't be fair, not on your terms. But it will be sublime, I can promise you that."

"Yes," she hissed, her "s" sibilant with lust. If he could make her go almost crazy with lust just by kissing her throat, what could the man do with his cock?

* * * * *

As they lay in the afterglow of their lovemaking Carly nestled against Jesse's smooth chest. The room was lit only by the silvered light of a fading moon, but it was enough to see the strong profile of her man, his thick dark lashes brushing the high curve of his cheekbone.

In the past when Carly finally worked herself up to sleep with a guy, and that wasn't often, almost the minute her orgasm had receded, doubts and recriminations would begin in her head. She would feel an itch, a need to escape. She chalked it up to her own apparent inability to connect. She blamed herself and felt she was "broken" in some way. She didn't know how to just *be* with someone. She had to analyze and ultimately destroy the moment.

Now she lay quietly, feeling the sweet, slow rise and fall of Jesse's chest under her head. His arm cradled her in an easy embrace. She realized with a little jolt of surprise she felt calm and serene. Instead of the usual patter ragging her brain—*What the hell did you just do? Why are you with this guy? How are you going to get out of here now? What if he wants you to stay all night?*—she felt a deep, quiet happiness that was entirely new.

Carly realized Jesse was asleep, though a moment before he had been murmuring sweet things to her. In a way she was glad he had fallen asleep because it gave her time to process what had just happened. Though she would never have considered herself submissive, whatever that even meant, he had been right when he said the experience would be "sublime".

Moving gently so as not to disturb her new lover, Carly reached back to touch her bottom. The skin was still tender from his hand. She shook her head a little. She couldn't believe she'd allowed this man to spank her! Like she was some kind of errant kid! And yet, she knew even as this thought flitted through her head that it hadn't been like that.

In fact it was far from it. She hadn't felt like a child when she had draped herself willingly over his strong thighs at his command, offering her ass up for a sensual spanking that left her weak with longing, despite or perhaps partially because of the sting. She had felt womanly and strong, and somehow empowered.

She didn't entirely understand the dynamic but perhaps that would come with time. She'd certainly read enough "submissive testimonials" online when she'd first begun preparing for her new job as a professional Dominatrix, but she realized now she had only skimmed the words with the barest of understanding, not really connecting on any meaningful level to what they meant.

The last few hours had turned Carly's world upside down. For the first time she had a gut-level knowledge of what it was to submit to another person—to freely give of yourself in a consensual exchange of power.

The events of the evening unfolded now in her memory and she let go, allowing them to play for her like a movie in her mind's eye. After she had agreed to try it "on his terms" things had moved rather quickly.

From the moment she had said yes, a change seemed to come over Jesse, though it was subtle. There was no longer a question in his touch, a hesitation as he waited to see if what he was doing suited his new lover.

His voice had a new authority as he said, "Take off your panties and your bra and put your hands behind your head, locking your fingers. Stand perfectly still so I can inspect you. This is typically called the 'attention position'. In the future, if we have a future, when I say 'attention', you will stand immediately and assume this position."

Jesse stared at her his eyebrow cocked a little, a hint of a smile at his lips. He was daring her to obey or to reject what he offered. Carly licked her lips, a mixture of raw fear and intense desire doing battle inside her. Yet through it all she knew intrinsically she could trust him completely.

Slowly she reached behind her back to unhook her bra, her fingers trembling slightly. Her high, round breasts bounced free. She slid her hands under the elastic of her panties at her hips, pulling the satin down smooth thighs until she stood naked before her dominant lover who was still fully clothed.

"Go on," he said, his voice low.

Her eyes locked on his, her face hot but not as hot as her cunt. Carly slowly lifted her arms, clasping her fingers behind her head. She was finding it difficult to get air and her breath came in little shudders.

Jesse moved close to her, tapping his foot against her inner ankle, forcing her to spread her legs. This one movement humiliated Carly—she felt like a cadet at a military school being corrected by her sergeant, or at least how she imagined that cadet might feel. Yet something kept her silent. She bit her lip in an effort to maintain her decorum. He had said to submit required strength and bravery, and she had a glimmer of what he meant. She didn't want to blow it now by protesting.

"That's better," Jesse said, standing back. "Now you look like a proper slave, awaiting inspection. If I owned you—" the words echoed in her head as he repeated them "—if I owned you, I would inspect you every morning like this. A master wants a slave who is properly groomed in every respect. I would make sure you were shaved in whatever manner suited me, and I would inspect my handiwork from the night before. I like to keep my slaves marked—a constant reminder of who they belong to."

Carly gasped as Jesse pulled her head back suddenly by the hair, his mouth hard on hers, nothing like the tender, heated kiss they had exchanged before. This was a claiming, pure and simple. He was establishing with this kiss his control over her—her body, her actions, her will. Carly found herself melting—that was just the word. She felt as if hot molten lava was coursing through her veins, leaving her on fire with passion and need.

When he finally released her mouth Carly moved forward like a babe still craving the breast. But instead of more kisses, Jesse pushed gently at Carly's shoulder. "Kneel," he whispered and she sank to her knees as if this was a natural position for her.

When Jesse opened his pants, allowing his thick, rigid member to spring free, Carly didn't need to be told what to do. Willingly, eagerly, she took the shaft between her lips, teasing his already hard cock until it was like iron, though the iron was covered in the soft, sweet satin of his skin.

As he pressed forward, she allowed him to use her mouth and throat, guiding himself into her as if she was a vessel created expressly for his pleasure. Instead of feeling used or debased, Carly found herself almost dripping with desire. Her fingers found her wet pussy, swollen and slick as he filled her mouth, the head of his cock lodged in her throat.

"That's it," he murmured, his voice thick with lust. "Take it just like that. I know you can't breathe right now. I know I'm blocking your windpipe. It's about trust, my love. I am so proud that you trust me right now. You don't pull back, you don't resist. You take what I give. When I have trained you properly, you'll be willing to pass out before you pull away, no matter what I do to you."

Carly shivered as these words penetrated her brain. Not only the promise — or threat — of what he would do to her, but the assurance with which he spoke about the future and the implication she would belong to him.

Slowly Jesse pulled back, his cock glistening with her kisses. As she watched, he pulled off his jeans and underwear and took off his shirt. His body was hard and smooth, a dark honey tan that made her want to lick him.

He pulled her up and into his arms and for that moment they were equal, his arousal evident in the rock-hard erection against her belly and in his kiss. Wrapping his arms around her, Jesse lifted Carly easily and carried her to his bedroom.

The bed was low to the ground, set in a black lacquered frame and covered in pale yellow silk. Jesse dropped her gently to the bed and knelt by the edge, pulling her body toward him so her legs were on either side of him. He leaned over, his tongue finding the sweet center of her, drawing sighs and moans as he suckled and gently bit the swollen, slippery flesh. It wasn't long before Carly was nearing orgasm. She was finally beyond modesty, finally beyond rational thought that would inhibit her natural responses.

Her breath came in little pants of ragged need as she started to arc over the sweet cascade of her orgasm. Suddenly his tongue was gone — that sweet velvet heat at her center was removed and she felt herself pulled back from the brink of release.

"What," she managed, her eyes opening. She wanted that tongue back *now*! Instead Jesse was kneeling back on his haunches, his cock still jutting out perpendicular to his firmly muscled abdomen.

"No," he said simply. "Not yet. Remember—my terms. That's my orgasm. That's my body. Just for tonight. You come when I tell you to and not a moment before, do you understand?"

As her passion began to recede, Carly became self-conscious of her pussy spread and swollen in front of this man. She sat up, closing her legs with a snap, her face a study in chagrin. She wanted to demand he pleasure her right now, and in just the way she wanted, or else!

But as their eyes met something happened—the connection between them, the fledgling link between sensual master and sexual slave was forged. Carly found her petulant irritation melting away. She understood on a primal level what he demanded. And she wanted to give it to him.

Slowly she lay back down. As his hand touched her thigh she let her legs fall open, the petals of her sex again offered to him. He licked her gently and then bit the tender flesh, just hard enough for her to feel the potential of his teeth, and then just a little harder. She moaned, something igniting inside her—something animal and needy.

As he alternated between teeth and tongue, Carly began to tremble, her body confusing pain and pleasure and somehow exalting in both. She knew she was near orgasm and also knew she wouldn't be able to control it, despite his admonition she wait for his permission. Luckily he relented, perhaps accepting the newness of her submissive status because he whispered between kisses, "Come now, my love. Come for me. Now."

And she did, arching and bucking against him, her cries a keening love song that she herself did not hear.

As her heart slowed from its wild beat and her breath finally sufficient for her to speak Carly whispered, "That was amazing."

Without conceit or the slightest trace of arrogance, but simply stating a fact, Jesse offered, "That was just the beginning."

And so it was. Jesse brought his new lover to orgasm over and over, until she was raw with sensation and covered with sweat. Skillfully he weaved acts of submission and pleasure, beginning to lay the circuitry so she would associate the one with the other, twisting pleasure with pain, weaving lust with obedience.

When he finally entered her for the first time at least an hour had passed, an hour where he had kept her teetering on the edge of orgasm until just the tip of his hard cock sent her screaming into a shuddering climax as she clawed his back in her passion.

Though she usually hated condoms, she couldn't even feel the one he'd slipped expertly over his rigid erection just before plunging into her wetness. Her lubrication more than sufficed to offset the little latex hood.

He grabbed her hands and held them high over her head against the pillows. "You're mine now, you see that, don't you? You belong to me. I've claimed you now. You are my lover, my whore, my slave, my angel." He thrust savagely into her, accenting each noun with a twist of his hips that sent her spiraling helplessly to yet another searing release.

At one point as they lay side by side on the rumpled sheets, Carly had whispered she needed to pee. Jesse had escorted her to the bathroom and watched as he forced her to relieve herself in the shower stall, her legs spread lewdly, the pale yellow stream hissing between them. A peculiar sexual shame had mingled with a still fierce desire as she committed this private act in front of her new lover. Another link in the D/s chain was forged as she endured this new humiliation.

He had taken her then on the bathroom floor, pushing her to the soft bath rug and mounting her from behind, though only thrusting a few times since he was unprotected and mindful of it. But just the dominant act of forcing her to the ground so he could fuck her, after watching her pee for his pleasure — it had been the crowning sweet humiliation. Instead of feeling shamed or horrified, Carly found herself exalted and almost wild with lust.

"Fuck me!" she had screamed, never wanting anything more in her life than she wanted his cock, right then, just as they were, kneeling naked on the bathroom floor. She had almost cried when he pulled out, tears burning her eyelids, her voice a plea for him to continue.

Refusing her he said, "You're a willful, demanding girl. You need to be taught a lesson. I'm going to teach you now." Pulling her up, he'd dragged her to the bedroom and sat himself upon the bed, patting his thigh.

"That's right—" he nodded "—time for your spanking, my bad little darling. Your gorgeous ass needs to be reddened to remind you that I am the one who calls the shots. You don't tell me to fuck you, you don't beg unless I want you to beg. You take what I give you and that's that."

Again he patted his leg as Carly stood in front of him. Her cheeks and chest were flushed, her nipples dark pink and distended, her eyes wild and dark, almost all pupil. The lust, which had painted her features, was now mixing with confusion and apprehension. A spanking?

"Now," Jesse ordered, his voice almost a growl. Despite her own fears, perhaps partially because of them, Carly found herself deeply aroused, if possible even more so than a moment before.

Slowly she draped herself over his thighs, feeling awkward and out of balance until he put a firm hand on the small of her back, steadying her. She leaned her cheek against his strong calf, inhaling his sweet, spicy scent. She could feel her own heart pounding wildly against his leg.

First his hands were feather-soft, the fingers dancing deftly over her skin, making it tingle with anticipation. She was surprised by the first swat, which stung, though not too much. Again the palm landed, flat against her tender ass.

"Ouch!" she squealed, for that time he'd hit her hard. Instead of stopping or massaging the area he'd just smacked, Jesse hit her other cheek just as hard. She imagined there must be a handprint of red against her white flesh. The image was somehow erotic and she shifted a little, trying to grind her clit against his knee.

Again and again he smacked her, until the sexual pleasure and excitement began to ebb in favor of real pain. This was too much! Carly began to whimper and writhe but Jesse held her firm with his hand. Her legs were locked between his. When she brought her hands back to protect her bottom, he slapped them away.

"Jesse! Stop! Really! You're hurting me!"

"That's the idea, little one. This is a punishment, not another way for you to masturbate against my knee." Even in her pain, Carly blushed though Jesse couldn't see her face. He smacked her several more times and she cried out with each blow.

Blessedly, just when she knew she couldn't take another swat, she felt his hands now gentle against heated bruised flesh. Softly he caressed the area he'd just spanked, soothing away much of the sting. Gently he lifted her from his lap and laid her on her belly on the bed.

She lay still, completely spent, her body feeling strangely as if she'd just had an orgasm instead of a spanking. The spanking had hurt, make no mistake about it, but a sensual pleasure had been there as well, weaving itself into the pain and confusing the fledgling submissive.

She jerked a little as something cold touched her tortured flesh. She realized it was cream and relaxed as Jesse massaged a soothing balm into her skin. "You were wonderful," he whispered beside her. "So brave. You took so much for a first time, my love. You are going to be a perfect sub. I know it in my bones. I can't believe I found you."

Carly's face was averted from his, but she beamed with his words, delighted she'd been brave and wonderful, thought it hadn't felt that way at the time.

Gently he turned her over and draped himself on top of her, his body's heavy sweetness comforting her like a quilt. This time when he entered her, he was gentle, his cock sliding smoothly into her velvet wetness as he kissed her eyelids, her cheeks, her mouth, her hair. "Carly," he whispered just before his cries became incoherent as he shuddered and bucked against her, filling the condom with his precious seed. For some reason that awareness made Carly sad, but it didn't stop her from coming a moment later herself, for the fifth or sixth time that night—she'd lost count.

Whatever it was she was discovering with this sexy dominant man, Carly knew she wanted to continue, no matter where it took her. Now as she drifted in a semi-sleep state of deep satiation, his words whispered through her brain… *This is just the beginning…*

Chapter Eight

ॐ

"Hank" became a regular, showing up like clockwork each Wednesday evening at Carly's door on the second floor of the club, with his head respectfully bowed. Eagerly he would strip out of his suit and tie, sitting docilely in the torture chair so Carly could strap him in. He also came on Monday mornings — Carly recalled now that her boss had usually left the office on Monday mornings, ostensibly to "check the warehouse".

The memory of her mean old boss had faded until she barely made the connection, even though it had only been a short time ago. This man, this submissive "Hank" seemed to have so little in common with the bully who had driven her from her old career. She no longer even wanted revenge against Mr. Franklin. Instead she tried to make Hank's experience erotic and special, though he wanted the same thing each and every time. She knew there was a certain comfort to the ritual, however bizarre it might be.

Carly had found a new appreciation for what her clients wanted. Having directly experienced that loss of control, which could transcend mere sexual experience, she found herself more sensitive to her client's desires and less quick to dismiss them as pathetic or twisted. As a result, though her outward actions might have remained the same, her connection on a primal level to her clients deepened and her popularity as a mistress soared. She could barely find enough hours in the day to dominate the many men and occasional woman who came her way, money in hand.

Pulling Hank's head back, Mistress Marlena, as she had become in the moment he walked into the room, hissed, "You need this, don't you, boy? You need to be tied down and cut with this knife. You need to suffer for your mistress, you nasty, dirty little cocksucker."

Hank thrived on this kind of talk, his cock thickening from her words. "Yes, Mistress, yes, please," he breathed.

"Shut up, slave!" She slapped him hard across the face. "I can see I'll have to gag you, you little pussy boy." Hank adored the rough treatment and the belittling language. He had brought a roll of silver duct tape for one session, asking that Carly gag him with it. He left the roll with her and it had become another ingredient in their little game. He would teeter on the edge of orgasm for the entire hour, often ejaculating before he was given permission, for which she would "humiliate" him with insults and further slaps to his jowly cheeks, invariably causing another erection in short order.

Now Carly tied him down securely, pulling the leather straps tight across his wrists, chest, thighs and ankles. She placed a piece of duct tape over his mouth as he moaned his approval. His eyes glinted with lust as she brought a very sharp thin blade close to his neck. She had learned not to come too close, as Hank had a tendency to jerk forward, finding the point of the blade and trying to draw his own blood if he could. The accident that first day had been quite enough for Carly and she had been careful to avoid a repeat performance.

One day several weeks into their "relationship", Carly had had to pee rather badly. She didn't like to leave her sub in the middle of a session, afraid it would ruin the mood, so she decided to try and incorporate her absence as a part of the game.

"You need to be punished. You're too impatient. I'm going to make you wait for what you know you deserve. I'm going to leave the room for ten minutes. When I get back that cock better be as hard as a rock or I'll have to whip it with my crop, you understand?"

Hank couldn't answer, gagged as he was with tape, but he nodded, his chest heaving, his penis straining between widely spread legs. Carly slipped out. After she used the bathroom, she checked her watch—she had said she would leave him for ten minutes. Why not take advantage of the time and check her schedule?

Carly hurried downstairs and went into the library. A new desk had been added for the new receptionist Anthony had hired. Actually he'd given her his old one and had a large fancy rolltop brought in from the parlor for his own use.

Now his desk was unoccupied as one of his clients had arrived and was being "tortured" down the hall from Hank. Mistress Julia was lounging on a couch, sporting in a black leather pantsuit and smoking a cigarette while she flipped through a magazine. She looked up briefly as Carly entered and then back down at her magazine. The new receptionist was there, too, sitting at her desk busily typing something on her keyboard.

"Hi, Marlena," she said brightly as Carly walked over to the little refrigerator by her desk to grab a cold soda. Anthony had been thrilled with Brittany who had answered his ad just one day after the "help wanted" sign had gone up in the front window. He had won his quest with Amanda for extra help at last and Brittany had seemed perfect for the job. References had checked out at the restaurant where she had been a hostess. She also gave a reference for some church, which Anthony didn't bother to check. Just the fact she had put it on her application must mean she was honest, he surmised.

She didn't seem too bright, but how smart did you have to be to answer the phone and the door, keep appointment books and do some light typing and simple data entry on the computer? Anthony still controlled the money and the books but Brittany's help with the other tasks had been invaluable to him in the two weeks she had been there. More than anything perhaps, was his sense of importance now that he had an assistant.

"Hi, Brittany—hi, Julia," Carly said.

"Aren't you working right now?" Julia asked, frowning.

"Yeah, just ran down for a soda and to check when my next appointment is. I'm trying a new thing—leaving him alone as part of his turn-on, all tied up and gagged and waiting for his torture to begin."

"Ah, very clever way to get a coffee break," Julia nodded her approval.

"Your next client arrives at twelve o'clock, Marlena," Brittany said crisply, holding Carly's appointment book in her hand and looking pleased with herself.

"Thanks, I couldn't remember if it was twelve or twelve-thirty. Well, I better get back up there before he goes ahead without me." Mistress Julia laughed while Brittany pursed in her lips in what looked like disapproval.

* * * * *

Edna had been right to suspect her husband of something shady. Still she had been stunned to realize just how shady, how utterly evil, his activities were.

Slowly she had come to suspect those so-called Rotary meetings were just a cover for something illicit. His disheveled appearance after the meetings and his overly solicitous treatment of her for the rest of the evening, no doubt born of guilt, began to make her suspicious. She half-expected to find lipstick stains on his collar or a phone number on a scrap of paper tucked into his pants. Such things had happened before, but she didn't find that sort of hard evidence this time. She would have to become craftier than he to catch him out.

The evening she had decided to follow him had been a real revelation. After he'd left her at the door of the Metropolitan Tabernacle Church, Henry had scurried off down the street as usual. Edna waited for a few moments in case he looked back to wave or something, but clearly his mind and intentions were elsewhere.

She followed, feeling excited and nervous at the same time. She knew she would feel foolish but relieved if he in fact went the two blocks west and one block north to the building where the Rotary Club meetings were held. She would miss part of the bible study but that couldn't be helped. She had her husband's soul to save!

There he was ahead, she recognized him walking very quickly. At the light he stopped and she waited, too, several yards back, her heart hammering in her chest. Now was the moment of truth—would he turn right and head on to his meeting, or not?

The light changed and Henry did not turn right. Instead he crossed the street in long strides, still going west, toward the "artsy" section of town. He was almost running now, a kind of loping canter Edna found hard to keep up with. Wherever he was going, the man was clearly in a hurry to get there.

She almost lost him for a moment when he turned a corner before she could catch up. There he was, up ahead. He stopped mid-block and stepped up onto a stoop, ringing a doorbell, his shoulders heaving as he no doubt labored to catch his breath. As she cautiously approached, she saw the door open and he disappeared inside.

Edna stood still, not sure for a moment what to do. She now knew with cold certainty her husband had been lying to her. Righteous indignation was now fighting inside her with trepidation—did she really *want* to discover just where he was going, just what he was doing? This must be the apartment of his latest floozy! Her first impulse was to turn and run. Why drag herself down into his filth with a confrontation?

Taking a deep breath, she thought of the Christian martyrs entering into certain death to stand up for what they believed. Surely she could muster enough courage to see where her lying weasel of a husband spent his Wednesday evenings!

Slowly she approached the old brownstone from the other side of the street. Instead of a row of doorbells with names taped next to them, as she had expected, she saw it was some kind of business establishment. A little sign painted in gold letters against a black oval was nailed up over the door. It read "Club de Sade". *What a curious name. What kind of place was this?*

She stood uncertainly on the sidewalk for a moment and then noticed a sign in the window, "Receptionist Help Wanted — Inquire Within". Edna slipped back into the shadows of a building as someone else approached the door. The man rang, waited a few moments and was admitted.

A whorehouse! Edna suddenly knew this must be some kind of bordello — a den of iniquity. If her father found out, he would throw Henry out of the company on his ear! Not that she would blame him! Though her father would blame *her* as well, she knew, for letting her husband stray from the fold. She did manage to drag him to church every Sunday, but she knew his heart wasn't in it. Henry was just as afraid of her father as she was, if not more so.

Later that evening as she sat in the church hall listening to the preacher talk of hellfire and damnation, and the duty to save the lost souls, she knew the sermon was directed at her. When it was over and people were mingling and visiting, Edna sat alone on a chair by the wall, thinking hard. She had to do something. Henry mustn't be permitted to sin like that anymore. She would gather more information though — line up her ducks before she made accusations. She needed to learn more about this "Club de Sade".

But how? She certainly had no intention of knocking on the door and entering a wicked house of sin! As she was musing a young woman walked up to her. "Hi, Mrs. Franklin. We missed you at bible study."

"What?" Edna was shaken out of her reverie. "Yes, I was, uh, detained. I had to go to the doctor's."

"Oh, I hope nothing serious?" Brittany Lane hovered solicitously around Edna. The young woman's voice was high and soft, reminding Edna of that tart Marilyn Monroe, as if she was all out of breath from fornication and God knew what else. Still, one couldn't help how one sounded, Edna told herself.

Brittany was an attractive young woman in her early twenties who came to the church for bible study and the sermon on Wednesday evenings. Edna disapproved of the way she dressed and the amount of makeup she wore, but knew she must be charitable. Even Jesus forgave fallen women.

Brittany didn't strike Edna as especially pious or religious but she gave her grudging points for coming to church at all. Most young people today had no time to think about saving their souls, intent instead on piling up the sins that would pave their way to hell.

Brittany had become especially friendly with Edna when she had learned of her close connections to the L. J. Smathers & Co. catalog company. Edna knew Brittany harbored a desire to be a model and an actress. She'd had some limited success with the former, appearing in local department store circulars. The little taste of fame had given her the idea she could "make it big". Meanwhile she worked at some restaurant and counted her pennies.

When she'd learned Edna was in fact the daughter of Mr. Smathers himself, Brittany had gushed, "Why, Mrs. Franklin! How fantastic! Do you think you could get me an audition for the women's clothing line? Shannon Long and Marilyn Drew got their starts in catalogs! And now look at them—fashion magazine covers, shoots in Europe, the whole nine yards!"

Edna didn't know who Shannon Long and Marilyn Drew were, but she knew naked desire when she saw it, and Brittany's face was a study in longing. Edna was not one to dispense favors idly. She put Brittany's request in the back of her mind. She could, in fact, call upon her father's good graces to get this girl a modeling interview. For that matter she could have Henry do it. At the time she had only said noncommittally, "You don't say."

Now as she looked up at Brittany a plan began to form in Edna's mind. She knew in her bones the Lord had something to do with it. Jesus had sent Brittany her way to do his bidding. "Brittany, how is your job going at the restaurant?"

"Oh, my God! I can't believe you said that! How did you know?" Tears appeared in Brittany's large brown eyes. "They let me go! Can you believe it? It's almost Christmas and I lose my income. I sure could use a catalog job now." She glanced hopefully at Edna.

"Well, I don't know. Though I have put out some feelers for you." *Throw her a bone*, Edna thought. She patted the chair next to her and said, "You know, sometimes the Lord works in mysterious ways. I do believe He has a plan for you. And for me. We have been given a task, Brittany. A task to save a soul."

Brittany's eyes widened. "Who?" she breathed.

"My lying, cheating, weasel of a husband, that's who," Edna snapped and then pursed her lips. She must control herself, she knew, or she might scare Brittany off. "Here's the thing, dear." She laid her hand on Brittany's arm. "My husband has strayed from the path of the righteous. He is on the road straight to hell and I mean to get him off it! He is sinning, Brittany. Sexually sinning. Right now, while you were sitting here listening to the word of the Lord, he was fornicating at some house of ill repute!"

"Really!" Brittany looked taken aback, her mouth open in surprise. "And what are we to do about it? How do we save him? What do I have to do with it?"

"Well, I know where he goes. It's not far from here actually. It's a place called Club de Sade. Here's the amazing thing. The part that made me know the Lord wants you to be a part of this. There's a 'help wanted' sign in the window! For a receptionist. You'd be perfect! See, I know I can't *make* him come back to the Lord. We have to be subtle about it. We have to line up our ducks in a row, as it were, and then, when the time is right, shoot them all dead!"

Brittany looked a little discomfited at this last outburst and Edna smoothed her dress over her knees, trying to calm herself. She needed Brittany as an ally if she was going to get the goods on Henry. She smiled at the young woman and said, "Figuratively speaking, of course. Here's the plan. You go and get that job. I know, I know—" she raised her hand as if Brittany were about to protest "—you'll be working in a viper's nest of sin. But think of Daniel and the lions! Think of Jesus with the lepers. You'll be doing the Lord's work, Brittany!"

"Gosh, it sounds like secret agent spy stuff!" Instead of looking horrified or frightened, Brittany looked interested, even eager. "I do need a job, that's for sure. But what would I be finding out exactly?"

"You would find out just what the place is, that's the first thing. And then you'd find out who Henry sees, what he does in there. Then when I confront him, he won't be able to deny it. He'll see that God has intervened, that God knows all and he'll repent."

"Well, I'm all for doing the Lord's work. And I have a Christmas list a mile long that isn't going to pay for itself. Are they open now?"

As Edna nodded Brittany added, "And you'll put in a word with your father for my modeling career." Brittany's usually breathy voice was suddenly hard. She wasn't asking a question, but stating a fact. Edna made a mental note to watch this one— she wasn't quite as flighty as she pretended.

"Bring your portfolio, Brittany. If you get the receptionist job, you can consider it done."

* * * * *

"I'm feeling a little weird about this, Mrs. Franklin. They're so nice over there. Are you sure it's a sin? I mean, I know it's a sin, but no one is being hurt or anything…" she trailed off under Edna's stern glare.

Edna sniffed loudly, refusing to dignify the foolish comments with a reply. The girl really was impossible. But she certainly was useful. The plan had dropped full-blown into Edna's mind, straight from a wrathful, but just, God she was certain. He wouldn't tolerate the abomination that was "Club de Sade" for long.

Brittany had gotten the job almost too easily. She was required to work some evenings, including Wednesdays. This further confirmed Edna's belief that the Lord approved of her intervention.

The stories Brittany brought back raised the hairs on the back of Edna's neck. Though Brittany had told her it wasn't a whorehouse, but more of a S&M play club — as if that was any better! — Edna hadn't been dissuaded. She knew evil when she saw it!

When Brittany described the tastes of a certain "Hank" whom Brittany confirmed came on Wednesday nights — a short man who hurried by the library office to meet with Mistress Marlena — Edna knew it was her husband. Her stomach actually hurt at the thought of his filthy perversions. Brittany was rather vague but said enough to confirm Edna's worst suspicions. Henry might well be past redemption.

She would get that den of filth shut down. "But it isn't against the law, you know. That's the amazing thing," Brittany had said. "As long as there is no exchange of bodily fluid —" Edna wrinkled her nose in distaste " — that is, you know, no sex —" Brittany whispered the last word " — then it's okay. It's kind of like a massage parlor, that's what Anthony told me. But the clients have, um, kinks. Not in their muscles, but in their libidos. I looked that up. It means —"

"I know what it means, thank you," Edna interrupted. Though it took a while, she was finally able to get a coherent picture of the place and its goings-on from Brittany. The girl did seem to have an eye for detail and Edna patiently extracted the information she needed — the layout of the place, the habits of its customers, most especially "Hank", the hours of operation and even details about the alarm system.

"Why, it sounds like you plan to break in or something," Brittany said, her expression quizzical.

"Don't be ridiculous. I'm merely lining up my ducks, as I've explained before. We've been thinking of getting an alarm system ourselves. You can't be too careful in the city, you know. You just input a code, right?"

"Yep. It's Amanda's dog's birthday. Isn't that adorable? I just got the code yesterday! I only have to remember four little numbers. Getting the code means I'm in. Permanent." Brittany looked proud but faltered suddenly, her expression clouding. "That is, I mean, do you really think it's a sin to work there? The money is fantastic. I make twice what I made as hostess and the job is a piece of cake! I was able to buy all my Christmas presents with money to spare!"

Edna didn't address the question directly. Of course, it was a sin, but sometimes the ends justified the means. Instead she said, "Her dog's birthday. That *is* adorable. What is her dog's birthday, anyway?"

"May first, nineteen ninety-nine. Oops!" Brittany looked stricken as her hand flew up to her mouth. "Rats. I promised Anthony I wouldn't tell anyone that code! Anyone! He trusts me." She held up her key chain by a key, presumably the key to the brownstone.

"Don't worry," Edna soothed as she eyed the key. "I'm no good with numbers. I've already forgotten what you said. Anyway, you probably have to punch it in, in a special way so I don't even know how to use the date, even if I could remember it. You didn't give me the code at all."

Brittany looked greatly relieved. "Well, that's good then. My big mouth is my best asset and my worst." She offered her best smile that showed her even white teeth to advantage, tilting her head slightly and shaking her long dark hair as if she was at a photo shoot. Edna forced a smile though it came out more as a grimace. She had to agree with Brittany. That mouth of hers could them both into big trouble. Time for phase two of the plan.

"I've been talking to my father, dear. It's taken a lot of persuasion but I think I can get you a modeling contract with the firm." As Brittany started to squeal with delight, Edna held up a hand. "No, no, don't thank me yet. You may not be interested. You see it would be in Chicago. That's where they do most of the layouts. They're already hard at work on the summer lineup. You would have to fly out within the next week or so, and plan to stay for at least a month. The company would put you up, of course. They own some apartments near their headquarters."

Edna had pressed hard for this one. She didn't ask much of her father—he was a forbidding man and not very approachable. But he had always had a soft spot for his "little girl" and she was careful what she asked for.

She'd painted the story of a beautiful young woman down on her luck, implying a "female illness" that she knew her father would not want to know the details of. Brittany's portfolio did show her to advantage and Edna's father had said, "I'll have my secretary call them at headquarters. What's her name again?" As Edna had answered, he said, "Consider it done."

Now Brittany's expression clouded. "Oh," she said. "I'd have to leave my job. After just getting settled in—"

Edna affected a stern expression. "Brittany! I'm shocked at you! Don't forget what our mission was! To save Henry from an afterlife of eternal damnation! You can't stay in that den of sin— it'll corrupt you."

"Oh, I don't know, it isn't so bad, really," Brittany tried, but Edna cut her off.

"See? Listen to you! Why, I think it's *already* corrupting you. You'd better get yourself out of there before you're past redemption yourself! And don't forget, this is a chance of a lifetime. The chance to make it big at last. To be on the covers of those magazines like those other famous models."

Brittany's eyes took on a starry look. Those last two words had reached her at last, even where fear of hellfire could not. Ah well, Edna could only save one soul at time. For now, she would get Brittany and her big mouth safely out of the city. Her dirty, nasty husband was going to be washed clean of his sins at last and Edna didn't need any witnesses gumming up the works.

Edna knew it was God's will when Brittany left her purse unattended as she went to use the restroom. The little key was easy to separate from the others and Edna pocketed it with a little smile as she turned back to listen to dear Reverend Johnson's words of inspiration.

Chapter Nine

ඐ

"Are you sure you want to try it?" Jesse whispered in Carly's ear. They were lying naked together in Jesse's bed, their bodies striped with sunlight slanting through the partially open blinds. The snow lay thick outside but the bedroom was warm and cozy.

Carly lay on her back, her eyes closed, the sheet covering the lower half of her body. Jesse stroked her breast, circling her nipple, which rose and darkened with the anticipation of his touch. He bent over her, lightly biting the little bud, drawing a moan from his lover.

He teased her for a while and then pulled away. Carly opened her eyes, her mouth forming a pout that clearly said she wanted more. "I asked you a question, Carly. I can see I'm distracting you from answering. In the heat of our lovemaking you said you wanted to feel the kiss of the lash. Last night you said you wanted to see what it was like to be whipped. I know we sometimes say things in the passion of the moment that we later wish we could take back. You still want to try it?"

"Yes. I want it. I think." Carly sat up, pulling the sheets up around her with body language that said she didn't know just what she wanted. Last night as he had made love to her, this time binding her wrists with soft rope and tying them to the headboard, he had whispered about the intensity of a whipping. About how it could feel like a hot, perfect kiss. The image of Angela, the sub who had been a part of his presentation back when she'd first seen Jesse on the stage, had risen in Carly's mind. How she stood so still and graceful as Jesse used that heavy flogger against her thin, delicate frame. And her expression afterwards—something almost religious in its ecstasy.

Even then, when Carly had had no understanding yet of her own submissive feelings and yearnings, she had been moved by that poetic display of submission and suffering. It was almost like some sort of erotic dance, which spoke directly to her own primal urges. Now she felt a tingling along her skin as if the whip's tresses were already teasing her.

Still, as she well knew, fantasy and reality could be very different indeed. It was one thing to take a spanking at the hands of her lover. A whip seemed a much more dangerous thing to contemplate! She shivered a little and hugged herself.

Jesse tilted his head, smiling slightly at her. It was as if he could read her thoughts, see her confusion. He didn't rush her for an answer. He never pressed her, she realized. Each step forward in the relationship had come because she was ready for it. This in itself was new for Carly who was used to men who pushed for what they wanted until they got it and usually ended up pushing her away in the process.

Jesse looked so adorable with his dark curling hair still sleep-tousled, his large expressive eyes regarding her tenderly, though there was an undercurrent of lust between them, which seemed to be a constant.

She felt reassured by his calm patience as he waited for her to frame her response. Jesse lay back on several pillows and beckoned for Carly to move into his arms. Stroking her mass of short, curly blonde hair, smoothing it behind her ear only to have it spring away again, he said, "I can see you aren't really certain, even though you say you want it. Remember, sweetheart, the foundation of any relationship is based on honesty and communication. This is even more paramount in a D/s relationship. Because of the nature of what occurs, you have to be free to tell me when something isn't right. When it scares you or is harming you in a way I hadn't anticipated. I'll be the one to decide if you're right, of course, but it's essential I have your open and honest input at all times. Otherwise it won't work."

This made sense to Carly. When it was just a one-hour "scene" like at the club, with the rules written out beforehand, trust and honesty didn't come into play, at least not much. It was a game, pure and simple, despite her efforts to imbue it with something more real.

"Well," Carly admitted. "I am a little nervous about it. I mean, I think want it. I keep thinking of Angela..." she trailed off, then added. "But what if I mess it up? I mean, what if I couldn't take it and I punched you or something?"

Jesse laughed. "You silly angel. I would never let it get to the point that you couldn't take it. We would start slow. We have all the time in the world, darling. You know, a sub doesn't spring full-blown from her master's forehead. It's a learning process. It can be very intense, though. Much more so than a 'vanilla' relationship, at least in my experience."

Warming to his topic, Jesse continued. "You really don't know how intense things can get. I've had subs who wanted to be pierced, even one who wanted to be branded. Some subs want to be slaves 24/7, to be told when they can eat, when they can pee, when they can sleep. That kind of thing isn't for me and I don't get the feeling that's your thing either."

As Carly vigorously nodded her head in agreement, Jesse grinned. "It's all about comfort levels. You go slow—you try things a little at a time and see if it works for you. Nothing is written in stone. There's no rule book. The only rule is that I, as your Dom, have the ultimate decision as to how far we go. You give up your freedom in that way, but only if that suits you. That is, if your nature truly is submissive, then it isn't something you give up reluctantly. It's something you long for, something coded in your bones that feels more natural than anything else in your life."

Carly answered slowly. "You know, it's weird. I never really had submissive fantasies. I mean, when I masturbated." She turned a little pink but continued. "The images in my head weren't of being tied down and whipped or anything like that. I never dreamed of being someone's sex slave, with no mind or will of my own. And yet, what we've shared these last weeks has been amazing. I know just what you mean, that it's coded in our bones. I feel so right, so natural with you." She leaned toward him and kissed the tip of his nose before continuing. "No one has ever reached me the way you have. Taken me somewhere so thrilling, so out of myself.

"Yes!" she went on, her voice more animated. "That's it. When you Dom me, you take me out of myself. In the past, I've always been so stuck in my own head. So focused on my feelings or my lack of feelings. On the way I'm coming across to my new lover, on how he is 'performing' for me. I know that sounds kind of superficial, but it's true. Maybe that's why I've never been able to connect with someone. I mean really connect. I've never been able to get out of my own head. But with you, it's like I'm flying. It's beyond my experience. Beyond words..." Carly trailed off, her expression dreamy.

Jesse answered softly. "You're right. There's something so powerful about a D/s relationship. Somehow, it goes beyond love. No, that isn't what I mean to say. It doesn't go beyond it—it augments it somehow. Makes it stronger. Like an alloy. When they mix metals and something much stronger is created than either element on its own. You want to know what I think about you experiencing your first whipping?"

"What?" she whispered.

"I think you're ready. Very ready. I think you'll fly like you've never flown before."

Carly answered him by kissing his mouth as she slid her naked body over his. His rising hardness was met by her eager wetness as she pressed down on his erection. She rode him like a stallion until he threw her over and impaled her with his cock, making her scream with pleasure as his hips danced and tilted just so until they both rocked in a sweet spasm of ecstasy. Just as she was catching her breath he said, "Stand at attention, Carly. I'm going to whip you now."

It was gentle at first. Just a kiss—his word—of the lash. The flogger he'd chosen from his arsenal of "toys" was the very one he'd used on Angela during his demonstration. The tresses were woven together in little braids of three. This made them pack more of a sting than an unbraided whip. Yet the tresses were of such soft suede that the first brushstrokes against her back felt merely sensual, like the brush of a lover's fingers.

Carly was standing naked in the center of Jesse's bedroom, her hands locked behind her head in the "attention" position. Jesse stood just behind her, naked as well, save for a pair of black silk boxers, which rode low on his hips.

For a moment he pressed up behind Carly, wrapping his arms around her torso, pressing his erection against the small of her back. Carly, eyes closed, sighed and pressed back against him. She started to drop her arms, to turn toward him but he stopped her, holding her still and placing her hands back in position.

Somehow this action, this small demonstration of control, aroused Carly further and she felt her pussy hot and moist between her legs. She resisted the urge to stroke herself, knowing at this moment that was surely forbidden.

As she stood quietly with this strong, sexy man behind her, she couldn't help but muse on the situation. Why was she doing this? Did she seek the pain? Was she a masochist, no different from Tommy or Hank or the other fellows she herself whipped on a daily basis?

It was ironic. She knew how to handle a whip, how to wield it so it wouldn't hurt too much, but could leave a welt, if that's what her sub boys wanted. Yet she herself had never felt the lick of a lash, the sting of leather finding its mark. Why did she want to now? *Did* she want to?

Part of herself, the thinking, rational part, told herself she was doing research—hadn't Jesse himself said it was important for a Dom to know what they were inflicting? To endure any sexual "torture" they were willing to mete out? She had been remiss in not experiencing this sooner!

But the sensual part of her, the part that bypassed the brain and went straight to her primal urges — that part wasn't thinking about furthering her education or her career. It wasn't thinking at all.

Her skin felt shivery — hot and cold at once. She could feel her heart beating a steady tattoo against her ribs. She could smell the hot leather of the whip. She could see her breasts rise and fall with her shallow, fast breathing but she couldn't seem to control it.

"Shh, slow down," Jesse whispered into her ear. He stepped back from her, saying in a soft, soothing voice. "You know you need this. Your body is aching to accept what your spirit longs for. You were born for the lash, my love. You were born for this."

He stroked her back with long sensuous sweeps of leather, preparing the flesh. It didn't hurt at all, in fact it felt rather lovely, like a caress.

Carly relaxed a little, some of the tension easing out of her taut body. She could do this! Gradually Jesse increased the friction, drawing back his wrist a little to get better leverage. Imperceptibly he increased the pressure until he was actually whipping his charge, the leather whistling a little just before it made contact with pale, soft skin.

Her head dropped back a little though her fingers were still dutifully locked behind her neck. Her mouth was slightly parted and she looked almost as if she was in a trance. Jesse chose this moment to move from the gentle initiation to something more substantial.

Carly drew her breath in sharply as she crossed the threshold from sensual to sting. Because of Jesse's skill, she had already withstood more than she would have thought she could, if a novice had been wielding the whip. As it was, he was whipping her steadily now, increasing the tempo and force until he drew a little cry of real pain from his sub.

"Oh! Please!" Carly managed to sputter. It hurt! It stung like a little fire of bees up and down her back, ass and thighs. Suddenly she wasn't so sure she liked this whipping. She had gone from feeling sexy and brave to feeling jittery and scared.

"I can't!"

"Of course you can, love. You're doing beautifully." Jesse continued to whip her back and ass, mostly her ass. He was using considerable force now, enough to make even a seasoned sub cry out.

Carly began hopping from foot to foot, shifting in a vain effort to avoid the constant rain of fire against her skin. Her fingers showed white-knuckled against the riot of her hair as she danced from side to side with each blow. Yet she didn't fall out of position. She didn't say, "Stop." She didn't turn around to face her torturer.

As the whip continued to slap her skin, which was now a glowing pink from shoulder to thigh, a curious thing began to happen. Carly's shuddering gasping breath seemed to slow. Her wildly pounding heart eased in her chest. The whip continued to strike her, just as hard or harder than a moment before, and yet she no longer felt the sting. Or more precisely, she still felt it, but it didn't hurt.

It felt wonderful. Her body was utterly relaxed. She felt as if a breeze could have toppled her and yet she stood still and erect, her head now completely back, her eyes closed, her lips parted, the same look of rapturous bliss on her face that had been on Angela's the day Jesse had whipped her onstage for all eyes to see.

"Yes," Jesse whispered, awe in his voice. "Yes." He struck her hard, almost savagely so she fell forward, her arms instinctively reaching out in front of her to break a fall. But she didn't fall. Instead she slowly stood herself upright again, her fingers gracefully catching each other as she moved back into position. He struck her again and this time her body absorbed the lash and she stood still, as graceful as a statue.

"My God, I knew you were a natural. You are beyond amazing. You're poetry in motion. *Te amo*. I love you." Jesse's voice cracked with emotion as he dropped the whip and moved in front of the beautiful naked woman who still stood, eyes shut, head back, arms raised.

Gently he pulled her fingers apart, lowering her arms to her sides. Catching her in a gentle embrace, he lifted her in his arms and moved her to the bed, lowering her carefully onto soft sheets.

Carly opened her eyes. The cool cotton of the sheets felt good against her burning back and ass. A kind of veil seemed to slip from her consciousness and it was if the world switched back on. The muffled whoosh of her own blood pulsing in her ears was replaced with the normal sounds of a car's horn outside, the clank of the radiator, her own steady breathing.

"What happened, Jesse? Something happened. I've never experienced anything like that."

"You were flying, Carly. I've never seen that happen the first time. Never. You are really something."

Carly grinned, tremendously pleased with both her lover and herself, though she still barely grasped what he was talking about. Jesse tried to explain. "I've seen it before, in well-trained subs. And I did think we could take you there, but not the first time! It's something that happens when you really let yourself become the experience—when you completely surrender yourself to the lash, to your master, to what you are."

Carly leaned up on one elbow, shaking her curls from her face. She wanted to understand but she felt so deliciously sleepy, like she'd just had a seriously fabulous orgasm instead of a whipping! She let herself drop back against the pillows and murmured, "Go on, tell me. I want to understand."

She did want to understand. None of her "sub boys" had reacted even remotely as she had. But then, as Jesse had told her, her experiences at the club had as much to do with true D/s as hooking had to do with true romance.

Jesse lay down on the bed next to her and said, "I get so jealous of submissives. We Doms only get to experience what you just went thought vicariously. It's like you're this soaring kite and we just try to grab on and fly with you, but in the end you're the one with the power. You're the one flying while we try to hang on."

Carly looked bemused to think of herself as the one with the power. Jesse asked, "What did it feel like? I saw it happening, but obviously only from my perspective. That moment when you seemed to move from suffering to utter peace. How did you do it?"

"I don't know exactly. It was like I couldn't take another stroke. I was about to scream. I knew I was messing it up and not being graceful and not 'taking it' or being brave, and then all of the sudden I *could* take it. No, it was more than that. I not only could take it, it was easy. I felt like something melted inside of me. Like something hard and tight I've been holding balled up inside all my life just sort of eased and…let go."

She nestled against Jesse. He said, "You know, that's not the first time I've heard that. The part about it being too intense, too much, and then suddenly you can take it. It's been described as 'submissive head space' or 'flying' but whatever you call it, it never ceases to amaze me. I've seen it happen mostly when the sub is experiencing something very intense. Something physically difficult to tolerate that challenges your grace and ability to submit. One woman told me it was like how she imagined heaven — that you had to go through a kind of purgatory before you could get to a place of freedom."

Carly didn't respond, silently wondering what woman it had been, jealousy pricking her. Jesse's kiss silenced her insecurities. After several delicious minutes Carly gently disengaged, sliding down the bed until her mouth was level with Jesse's crotch.

Teasingly she licked and bit at his cock through the black silk of his boxers. She felt his member stiffen and jut toward her, still trapped in fabric. "Pull them off," he managed gruffly, arousal stopping his throat.

She didn't need a second command, sliding the silk past the sweet indentations just below his hips and letting his gorgeous cock spring erect in its nest of soft curls. It was long and thick, the soft, spongy head gleaming with a drop of pre-cum. Slowly she slid her lips down his shaft, keeping her eyes open and on his as she did so. He moaned and his dark eyes flashed with lust.

Now Carly was indeed certain of her own power as she drew Jesse closer and closer to his own release. She felt him stiffen and elongate in her mouth and she consciously relaxed her throat to fully receive him.

She was just about to bring him to a climax and she was very turned on by his obvious arousal. Suddenly he pulled back, taking his delicious cock from her. She pouted as if she was a little girl and he'd just taken her lollipop.

"Hey," she said, half-teasing, half-serious. "Give me that back!" Ignoring her, Jesse pressed the naked girl back against the bed. Taking her wrists easily in one hand, he lifted her arms above her head. She forgot her protests as his mouth found hers.

Between kisses Jesse murmured, "Do you belong to me, Carly? Are you mine?"

"Yes, oh, yes," she whispered back ardently, searching for his lips with her own and pulling him down onto her and into her. There was no master and no sub when their bodies joined, just two lovers reveling in each other and in the moment.

* * * * *

"No way!" Eva expostulated, just before taking a healthy bite of her corned beef sandwich. The girls had let their weekly lunches slide since Carly had quit her office job. She was glad they were meeting up again. She didn't want to lose her old friend.

"What do you mean, no way? You're the one who was so gung ho about all this in the first place." Carly felt embarrassed and self-conscious at Eva's reaction. She had confided about the intense D/s experience with her new lover Jesse. She hadn't expected Eva's reaction to be anything but admiring and excited. Perhaps she'd changed more in the past few months than she'd realized.

"Well, yeah. As a gig, as a way to make money. And with *you* being the one holding the whip! What did he do, tie you up? And you *let* him? Ms. Carly-Liberated-Woman-Don't-Touch-Me-I'm Emotionally-Unavailable-Stevens?"

Carly laughed despite herself. "Oh, stop. I'm not as bad as all that."

"Since when? I've seen you reject guy after guy because his shirt wasn't right or he laughed wrong at your joke. I *never* thought I'd see the day when you'd put yourself in such a vulnerable position with a man!" She leaned forward, her expression earnest now. "But seriously. It sounds amazing. Dangerous. This guy sounds super-hot and sexy. When do we get to meet him? The man who broke through the ice around Carly Steven's heart?"

Carly took a drink of her tea, giving herself time to compose her thoughts. She was still focused on Eva's earlier comments. "Was I really that shut down? That remote?"

"Absolutely. George and I despaired of ever seeing you in love. I'd marvel, because you're so beautiful—" Carly blushed and shook her head as Eva continued "—that men weren't breaking down your door. But George told me it was because you were shut down. You sent out 'not available' vibes that guys can pick up on. Still, I never thought you'd end up being *submissive* to some guy, for Pete's sake!"

"Well, up until I got into all this, I would have agreed with you. But you're confused in the same way I was at first. Being sexually submissive and being intellectually and socially liberated are *not* mutually exclusive states of being. You know, if you really think about it, it takes courage and a certain confidence to be able to submit. To make the decision to give that power to another person voluntarily."

"Sounds fancy," Eva said, grinning. "But what's it *feel* like? That's what I want to know. What's it like to be tied up, naked and helpless, while a man spanks your bare bottom and then has his way with you?" She hugged herself, licking her lips, not looking in the least horrified at the prospect.

A couple at a nearby table turned to look curiously at the two young women, having clearly overhead this conversation. The girls both glanced at the couple and then back at each other before bursting into uncontrollable laughter.

Chapter Ten

∾

Is ten minutes all it takes to destroy a life? Two lives?

Carly stood frozen in horror just inside the door of the blue room, the room where she'd been successfully Domming submissive, masochistic men for the past several months with no mishaps. For a second she thought it was some kind of joke. A sick joke, but a joke nonetheless.

At first she couldn't understand what lay before her. Hank was still strapped in the chair just as she had left him a few minutes before, naked save for the sleep mask blindfold and a piece of duct tape across his mouth.

But instead of eagerly waiting for his mistress's return, Hank's head was lolling at an odd angle against his shoulder and his throat was slit from ear to ear. Blood covered his body, snaking down his chest and paunch, still trickling down his legs to form a little puddle on the floor between his bound ankles.

Carly was dimly aware of a sound. A high-pitched scream that wouldn't stop. The room was getting dim and gray and she felt sick to her stomach, her gorge rising with nausea and terror. The scream stopped when she crumpled to the floor in a dead faint.

* * * * *

"What happened? What's going on?" Carly's head was throbbing and she couldn't get her bearings. Anthony was kneeling next her, his face a mixture of concern and relief. "God, Carly. What the hell happened? The police are on their way. When I heard you screaming I thought one of the clients had gotten out of control. We've never had anything like this! Jesus, this is going to close us down."

She was lying on a bed in the room next to one where presumably Hank still sat, held upright by the bindings Carly had placed upon him. "Anthony. I don't know what happened! Oh, my head." Carly sat up in the bed and touched the lump that had risen on her forehead. She moaned softly as the image of Hank, bound and bloodied in the chair, rose before her eyes.

"Well, there's a dead man in your room, Carly. I can't believe I'm even going to ask this, but—" he hesitated "—did the knife slip? Did you kill him?"

"God, Anthony. God, no! How can you even ask me that?" Carly found she couldn't catch her breath. Her eyes were filled with tears and she felt sick again. Weakly she slid back against the pillow.

"I'm sorry, hon. I won't be the last one to ask you that, you can be sure. Like I said, the police are on their way." He patted her hand solicitously. "Was it an accident? Too close with the knife? I know Hank was into knife play in a serious way."

"Stop it! I said no! He was like that when I came back upstairs! I just went to the bathroom and then got a soda, as usual. It was part of our game, our ritual. I would leave him for a few minutes and when I would come back he would be raring to go, all the more excited from the anticipation I guess. When I left him he was fine, just fine…" she trailed off miserably, her arm thrown over her face.

There was noise below and Anthony said, "Look, just take it easy. I have to get down there. Just hang in there, Carly. I believe you. But *someone* killed Hank, which means we have a murderer around here! Jesus, Amanda is going to die. Oh, man, what's gonna happen…" he continued talking to himself as he scurried down the hall, leaving Carly alone in the darkened room.

* * * * *

Jesse stared at the receiver, trying to process what he was hearing. He'd been awakened out of a deep sleep by the phone ringing. It was well past midnight. He felt as if he had been struck physically, so stunned was he by her words. Carly was on the other end.

"I'm down at the police station. I'm being held for questioning for a m-m-murder." Carly choked back the tears that were threatening to spill over. "They've been grilling me for hours. They said I can go home now, but it's so late, I don't want to take the subway or the bus. I thought you could come get me." She choked back a sob as the police officer standing next to her glanced her way, as if waiting for her to finally break down.

"Jesus, Carly. What's happened! Wait, don't tell me now. You must be exhausted. Thank God, you're safe! I called earlier and wondered when you didn't return the call. Just wait for me—I'll be there as fast as I can."

Jesse's heart surged with pity and love as he saw Carly huddled on a bench in the station's waiting area. Even though it was three in the morning the place was active, with a few miserable-looking men and women, some still in cuffs, waiting their turns to be processed into the "system".

They weren't as lucky as Carly who had only been questioned for several hours by two tired-looking detectives. They'd brought her into a small, overheated room and left her there for about twenty minutes, during which she sat in a numbed daze, still barely able to comprehend what was happening.

When they'd finally joined her, they actually brought her a cup of tepid brownish liquid which was supposed to pass as coffee. But when she'd tried to sip it she'd felt her gorge rise and her throat close. With trembling hands she'd set it down and held it cupped between her palms.

Over and over they questioned her about her whereabouts and actions at the time of the murder. At first they tried to get her to confess, but when it became clear she wasn't going to admit to anything, they switched tactics, focusing on her "career" as a Dominatrix.

Their expressions were sly and knowing as they pressed her for the details of her activities with her clients. Carly's face burned with embarrassment as they forced intimate information about her sessions. Several times she said she wanted a lawyer, and they responded that she wasn't under arrest — what was she afraid of?

"If I'm not under arrest, can I go now? It's well after midnight and this has been the most horrible night of my life. I'd really like to get home."

"A few more questions, ma'am, then we'll be in touch." Then they'd start again, covering the same ground over and over, probably trying to trip her up or catch her in a lie.

When they finally let her go, she was permitted to use her cell phone. As she flipped it open she thought for a second that she should call Eva. Did she want to involve her new lover in this mess? But her fingers decided otherwise, pressing the speed-dial number for Jesse's cell phone.

Now, as Jesse glanced over at her, she looked fragile, drained of all strength. Gently he touched her knee as they drove the short distance to her apartment. The winter sky was a leaden gray. Mercifully, due to the early hour, traffic wasn't bad and soon he was escorting her into the rickety old elevator up to her efficiency apartment.

Jesse sat Carly at her little kitchen table while he put on the kettle to boil some water. Wordlessly he prepared her a cup of hot black tea with lemon, just as he knew she liked. She took a sip and he noted her hand was trembling as she held the mug.

He slipped into the chair across from her and said softly, "Tell me what happened."

Slowly at first, then with the words tumbling from her, Carly outlined the horrible nightmare of the past hours. Jesse listened, his eyes narrowed in concentration. Unlike Anthony and the detectives, he didn't ask Carly if she'd done it.

Instead, he put his strong, warm hand firmly over hers and said, "You've been through hell, sweetheart. What you need is a good night's sleep. Then in the morning, I'll get right on this. I've got contacts in that precinct, in fact the captain there is a friend of mine. I'll be able to get an inside handle on the investigation and I plan to do a little investigating of my own."

He continued, his voice calm and reassuring, "Obviously, they don't have enough evidence to arrest anyone, meaning you, or they would have. The fact they only brought you down for questioning, and didn't try to hold you as a material witness, definitely works in our favor."

He squeezed her hand gently and said, "This is my domain. I don't do murders as a general rule, but I know the procedures and I know people in this city. We'll catch the real killer and clear your name, I promise you."

Carly smiled bleakly, bending her head as tears spilled down her cheeks. Jesse leaned over the table and wiped a tear with his finger, his face a study in compassion. Looking up at him Carly said quietly, "Thank you. Thank you for knowing I didn't do this horrible thing. Anthony actually asked me. The police as much as accused me. All they saw was this hooker, that's what they said, this hooker dressed in leather. Guilty by association, guilty by profession. Thank God, they let me change back into my regular clothes before they took me in the squad car."

"Did they cuff you?"

"No."

"Well, consider yourself lucky. They certainly could have. They would have if they really thought you were a dangerous murderer." He patted her hand and sighed. "We can certainly see it from their perspective. He was your client and he was killed with your knife, in your room. You were the last person to see him alive, other than the murderer of course. They're going to look into his life and into yours. See if they can come up with any motive for you killing him. Of course they won't find one."

The light vanished from her face. "Oh, my God…" she whispered.

Jesse felt a jolt of panic. The tiniest shard of doubt slid across his thoughts but was instantly dispelled. Carly was not a murderer. But what then? He had to know if he was to help her. "Carly. What is it? You need to tell me everything. We'll go together to the precinct and we'll tell them all you know. It could help Hank. That is, it could help them solve the crime. What is it? Is there something about the two of you?"

Carly took a deep breath and let it out slowly, then lifted her eyes to meet his. Her voice shook. "Hank aka Henry Franklin was my boss. My ex-boss. I quit just before he fired me. We had a huge fight and I walked out. Everyone in the office knew about it. That's why I got into this Dominatrix thing in the first place. I wanted to try something totally new. At first it was just for fun, but I found I was really good at it. And the money is great. When Hank, that is, my old boss, came in and I was asked to step in for his mistress who hadn't shown up for the appointment, he was as surprised as I was!

"But I guess it was part of the thrill for him. He liked to be humiliated. Degraded. I guess it worked right into his fantasy to have someone he used to have power over now with power over him. He knew he'd be safe because our confidentiality rules are sacrosanct. We'd be out of business in a New York minute if they weren't."

"That is a bizarre coincidence, Carly." Jesse looked grave. "It would almost be funny except for the fact that it gives you a motive. Revenge."

Carly gasped, her hand flying to her mouth. "But I didn't want revenge! It was weird, but after the first shock, I found I barely thought about our old relationship. I was Mistress Marlena now, and he was Hank and that old anger I used to feel just seemed to fade away. It all seemed so insignificant somehow."

Jesse pursed his lips and thought a moment. "Well, this definitely thickens the plot, but that just means we'll need to find out all the quicker who wanted him dead, and why. It could be a random killer, but that seems unlikely, given that the murder occurred inside the club. It's kept locked, isn't it?"

"Yes, we all have keys, though. All the staff that is. And we know the code to the alarm box. I don't know how anyone else could have gotten in. My God, that means someone there, someone I know, did this horrible thing!" Carly eyes were wide.

"That could well be. But not necessarily. Someone else could have gotten hold of a key and learned the code. Whoever it was, we'll find them, Carly. I'll find them. I won't let anything happen to you." He spoke with a confidence he didn't entirely feel. Yet he knew he had to do what he had promised or Carly might well be facing trial for a murder she didn't commit.

* * * * *

"I'll be blunt with you, Hernandez. Right now she's our number one suspect. Of course we've only been at it a few hours." Captain O'Reilly pushed his iron-gray hair from his forehead with an unconscious gesture he probably did a hundred times a day. His expression was grim but his eyes were kind.

Jesse and Frank O'Reilly who headed up the precinct where Carly had been taken for questioning, went back a number of years to when O'Reilly was still a detective. While they weren't personal friends, they had a good working relationship. Jesse had always cooperated with law enforcement when cases he was working on involved them. And more than once, he had helped O'Reilly solve crimes without ever seeking credit for himself.

Now Jesse said, "She didn't do it. I'm sure of it." Jesse leaned forward. He had decided it would be better for him and the captain to meet alone, without involving Carly. He'd left her sleeping that morning, still exhausted from her ordeal the night before. Grazing her forehead with a kiss, he slipped out of her apartment carefully locking it with the spare key she'd given him. There was, after all, a murderer still out there who had killed once and might kill again.

Jesse hadn't mentioned the fact to her that Carly herself might be at risk with the killer still on the loose. He hoped to spare her as much as possible. He knew her ordeal with the police was far from over.

"So what exactly is your interest in this case, Hernandez? This hooker a friend of yours? I gotta tell you, right now it doesn't look good for the little lady."

"Stop right there. She's *not* a hooker and you know it. Even if she was, that doesn't make her more suspect than any other person, or it shouldn't. But that aside, you know the Club de Sade is a legitimate play club duly registered with the City of New York. You know it abides by all the laws pertaining to that sort of place, and that no sexual acts are performed and no bodily fluids are exchanged."

"You seem to know an awful lot about it, Hernandez," O'Reilly remarked sardonically.

"I know a lot about a lot of things, O'Reilly," Jesse responded smoothly. "And to answer your earlier question, yes, she's a friend of mine. A *very* good friend."

O'Reilly grunted as Jesse continued, "Carly hasn't broken any laws. What she did was provide a service. Admittedly, a rather bizarre service, given our puritanical and rigid societal mores." Now O'Reilly grinned. Hernandez was on a roll, and he was famous for his lectures about "society". But he listened as Jesse said, "But here's the thing, Frank. The potentially complicating factor. Carly knew the victim. They knew each other before they had a, uh, professional relationship."

"Did they," O'Reilly said without inflection as he sat back, lacing his fingers over his ample girth.

"Yeah. They did. She used to work for him."

"You don't say. In what capacity?"

"A clothing catalog company. He was her boss."

"Interesting. And they parted amicably?"

"Well, no. See, that's the thing. They didn't get along and she quit. Apparently it wasn't a friendly parting. But that was all water over the dam by the time they started this new relationship."

"Uh-huh," O'Reilly said. "Like I said, this doesn't look good for your girlfriend, Hernandez."

Despite what the captain said, he was a professional and knew every angle had to be pursued before sufficient evidence could be gathered to arrest Carly for murder. They were still questioning all the people on the premises at the time of the murder. And he well knew in many of these cases, it was the spouse or a close family member who did the killing.

Following the same line of reasoning Jesse asked, "What about the wife? Have you questioned her? Does she have an alibi?" O'Reilly had informed him she was a regular churchgoer. *Not a hooker like your girlfriend* was the implication. They had been married for fourteen years and the wife had seemed sincere in her distress upon learning about the death of her husband. She had also acted justifiably horrified to learn of the circumstances.

O'Reilly flipped through some notes on a legal pad, until he found what he was looking for. "Yes, she has an alibi, though not airtight. She attends a church bible study group every Wednesday night and was there last night when he was murdered. As yet, we haven't found anyone who can absolutely verify she was there at the precise time of the murder, which the coroner has confirmed to be between 8:30 and 9:00. People saw her at the beginning of the meeting and they saw her at the end of the evening, after the pastor's sermon, which followed the bible study."

"Where's this church located?" Jesse interjected.

"About six blocks from the Club de Sade as a matter of fact. It's just possible that she could have hightailed it over there in the dead of winter, slipped inside the club, slit her naked husband's throat while he was tied to a chair and slipped away, all unobserved, and made it back in time to hear the sermon like a good Christian." Put that way, it did sound ludicrous.

"It was the knife wound then, for sure, that killed him? Not a heart attack or something?"

"No question about it. It looks almost like a professional job. A sharp knife was used, with a six-inch blade. Your girlfriend's, uh, playing knife. Part of her 'toy kit' so I understand."

"That stuff belongs to the club. It's always kept in that room for the clients who like that sort of play."

O'Reilly grunted and made a face before continuing. "The blade was inserted in his throat, dead center, probably to sever his vocal cords. The slit extended to the right, neatly cutting the carotid artery. In a matter of seconds, he had bled to death. It really doesn't sound like something a middle-aged churchgoing woman would do, not any of it."

"I admit it sounds pretty unlikely," Jesse conceded, his heart dropping. "But stranger things have happened. Has her house been searched? Did they find anything?"

"Yes and no. That is, no weapon as we already have the murder weapon, your girlfriend's knife. Nothing suspicious. Just a regular brownstone condo. Ritzy. They obviously weren't hurting for money. Her father's the one with all the dough. As far as we know at this point, she's not any better off financially by having Franklin out of the picture, except for a small life insurance policy provided by the catalog company. No motive, no weapon. Nada."

"You don't mind if I do a little investigating on my own, do you, Frank? I promise not to step on any police toes and I'll turn over any pertinent information the minute I find it."

"Go ahead, Jess. I trust you. We've only just started, obviously, in our investigation. I'll share what I can, as long as it doesn't impede the investigation. Here's the address of the church and the wife. We really don't have a hell of a lot more than that at this point ourselves. My men are focusing on that sex club at the moment. The scene of the crime."

Jesse pulled out his own little pad and was busily copying down the information when he was interrupted by O'Reilly's warning. "I'm rooting for you, buddy. But don't let your feelings get in the way of good investigating. You might well be too involved in this to see things clearly. You might end up doing more harm than good for Carly. We're going to be tearing her life apart to find out the truth."

"The truth or an easy solution to your case?" Jesse spoke more harshly than he had meant. He swallowed and took a deep breath. He knew O'Reilly's warning about letting his feelings get in the way of good investigative skills was true. He was in love with Carly and he knew in his bones she was innocent. But he owed it to her to do the best job he could without glossing over anything that might look at first as if it could harm her. The truth would exonerate her, he was certain.

Now there was just that little detail of discovering the truth. He had to move fast, before the trail ran cold. The police seemed convinced of Carly's guilt and thus weren't pressing too hard along other lines. It would be up to him to save the woman he loved.

* * * * *

Jesse had found the Metropolitan Tabernacle Church, the church Mrs. Franklin had given as the location of her alibi the night of the murder. It had been easy to walk into the non-secured building in the middle of the afternoon, though they probably locked the doors come nightfall. It was an old stone church with a high steeple, wedged between more modern red brick buildings that had gone up around it over the decades. Jesse had looked around the small empty chapel, its pews stiff and high, facing a highly detailed Christ, bloodied in agony on the golden cross over the altar.

He had stepped into a side room, which was more like a classroom, complete with tables and chairs arranged in patterns around the room suggesting various meetings or classes might take place at the same time.

"Hello?" he had called out in a friendly tone. "Is anyone at home?"

A tall, rather elegant-looking man with silver hair brushed back from his high forehead had stepped out from a small office. "May I help you?" he said in a deep sonorous baritone, perfect for a preacher Jesse had thought. A timid-looking washed-out little woman stood just behind him, her hands clenched nervously in front of her.

The idea that he was a reporter doing a story on church architecture in the city had come easily to Jesse. An hour at the public library had armed him with enough knowledge, he hoped, to seem genuine in his interest.

In his line of business he was known to assume any number of identities and was knowledgeable enough of each to be convincing, at least for short periods. While a khaki-colored jumpsuit with a name stitched over the heart and clipboard in his hand usually put most people at ease, that day he had been wearing a suit and tie, a stenographer's pad at his side and an earnest look on his face.

It hadn't been hard to convince the good Reverend he worked for *The Christian Review*, a prominent, local religious paper. He had flashed a formal-looking ID badge, not giving the man too long to read it as he said, "The Metropolitan Tabernacle has quite an impressive history, Reverend Johnson. I'm writing a story on some of the more elegant churches in the area and I'd love to get your perspective."

That was all it took. The minister and his secretary had eagerly shared their knowledge of the history of the church and their own involvement in maintaining its resplendence. They were clearly quite proud of their building and Jesse learned more than he wanted to. Smiling and asking questions, the answers to which he pretended to write on his pad, he slowly moved the conversation toward what he was really after.

"You know, I'm always so impressed with how the church is such a place of solace for people in times of distress. A safe haven to come to when all else seems so dark." The silver-haired minister nodded sagely as Jesse had continued. "I'm thinking specifically at this moment of poor Mrs. Franklin. She is a member of your fine congregation, is she not? Of course, being a newsman, I'm aware of the tragic murder of her husband. How's she holding up?"

"Well, uh, under the circumstances, she's doing remarkably well. A good Christian woman with her faith to buoy her up in times of need."

"Yes, of course. That's excellent news. You know," Jesse had paused and looked up from his pad as if the idea were just occurring to him. "I just had a thought! Wouldn't this make a terrific story? I'd love to do an article about how people's faith carries them along when all seems lost. Think how inspiring it could be!" Jesse tried to infuse his words with evangelical inflection, hoping at the same time that he wasn't overdoing it.

It was the secretary who had been introduced to him as Miss Hammond who had answered excitedly. "Why, yes! That's a wonderful idea. I can tell you all about that. I lost my husband to cancer ten years ago. If it wasn't for this church—" she had paused, looking adoringly for a moment at the dignified preacher who seemed completely unaware of her attentions "—I don't think I'd have made it through."

"Marvelous," Jesse had breathed, though he had no intention of wasting more time pretending to interview this poor woman for an article, which would never be written. Feeling a twinge of guilt he said, "I'd love to come back and do that story with you, if I may, Miss Hammond."

As she had nodded happily he continued, his voice subdued, "About the Franklins. Tragic, just tragic! What is the world coming to?"

"Why, yes, a bizarre and unfortunate situation." The minister looked extremely uncomfortable. Clearly he'd seen the article in the paper, with its description of the "S&M Dungeon" where the victim had been found. The details had been sparse, as the reporter who had gotten hold of the story hadn't been able to get much information yet. Jesse was sure they would soon though, as the story had all the lurid appeal of a tabloid attention grabber.

Jesse saw the reverend's discomfort and made his pitch. "I think Mrs. Franklin would be just the sort of person who could most benefit from the loving arms of her church right now, don't you? Perhaps her story, unfolding now as the police work diligently to solve the crime, would be all the more poignant."

Of course, he hadn't needed their permission to talk to the wife—he knew her address from the police records, but this gave Jesse a cover if Mrs. Franklin decided to investigate his credentials more thoroughly than these two trusting souls had.

Now Jesse took a sip of the coffee his hostess had offered him without tasting it. He set the fragile bone china cup back into its saucer on the coffee table and flipped open his notepad. Jesse was sitting in Edna Franklin's living room, again under the false pretense he was a reporter for *The Christian Review*. She had been hesitant to let him in at first, assuming he was another policeman come to harass her.

"I heard of your loss, Mrs. Franklin, through Reverend Johnson. He sends his deepest condolences."

Edna pursed her lips and arched her eyebrows in surprise. "Reverend Johnson! Have the police been there, too? Is nothing sacred?" Yet she opened the door enough to let him enter. The mention of the reverend was apparently enough.

Jesse thought he detected the slightest note of fear in her voice. *What was she afraid of?* He said soothingly, "Oh, it's just routine, I'm sure. You see, I'm working on a different article on the architecture of some of our old churches. While I was talking to the reverend about it we began to discuss how it is that the church can give us such comfort and succor in times of greatest need. If it isn't too indelicate, I was hoping your story could be the main feature of our paper, Mrs. Franklin."

He lowered his voice respectfully and added, "Your dearly departed husband probably took comfort from the church too, and now he's nestled in the bosom of the Lord."

"Hmph!" Mrs. Franklin snorted. "I couldn't drag him to that church except on Sunday mornings and even then he'd fall asleep halfway through—" She stopped suddenly, perhaps aware of how this little tirade sounded about a man who had just been murdered, a man she was supposed to have loved.

Jesse betrayed nothing in his face, instead smiling sadly. "It sounds like you've had your own crosses to bear even before this terrible tragedy. Your story could inspire others. I envision the article as exploring how your faith helps you through this trying time. You must miss him terribly. Despite his wicked ways."

"Oh, yes," she nodded absently and her eyes flickered away. *She was lying. She didn't miss him! Not at all. So much for the doting wife stricken at the murder of her poor husband. She seemed almost satisfied—as if he'd gotten his just desserts.* Still, that didn't make her a murderer. Jesse knew he would need more than a feeling to take to the police.

They talked on for a while as he pretended to take notes about her views on hell and damnation, about which she had very decided opinions. What emerged was an angry and rigid woman who felt cheated by life and who had resorted to religion for solace. For a moment Jesse felt almost sorry for the woman, but mostly he was repelled by her narrow-minded intolerance for anyone who did not believe exactly as she did about salvation and the path to it.

With subtle encouragement on his part, she became more open about her real feelings toward her dearly departed husband. "Well, Henry was a sick man, there's no question. A decadent, perverted soul with twisted urges and desires. But I never dreamed he'd stoop so low as to get involved with whores and criminals. He came to a bad end. I always knew he was on the road to hell. May God save his soul. I know I couldn't."

Jesse started at that last remark. *I know I couldn't.* An odd remark—it implied she had tried. And when she found herself unsuccessful, did she take matters into her own hands? Did the end justify the means? To what end was she willing to stoop to save Henry from himself?

That night Jesse stayed at Carly's apartment. Until the murder they had always stayed in his more spacious place, but Carly felt more comfortable right now with her own things around her. In some ways it was like a hiding place in the midst of a war.

Over Chinese takeout they talked for a long time, going over and over what might have happened and who might have done it. Eventually Jesse tried to change the subject but Carly was obsessed. It was almost as if by talking about it she could keep the frightening reality of her predicament at bay, or at least feel as though she was doing something about it.

"You know, Jesse, without you I'd be totally lost right now. It's so incredible that you're going to be able to help me. I mean, you could have been a scientist or a doctor or a sanitation worker. How incredibly lucky am I that you're a private detective? With your help, we'll be able to solve this! You'll be able to make sure those detectives don't go off on wild goose chases."

She clung to him then in a gesture that belied her brave words, tears making her large blue eyes sparkle and wrenching his heart anew. He desperately hoped her confidence in him wasn't misplaced, and he would be able to break the case soon, before they put her through more grueling questioning.

It was late and they were both tired, though Carly was still keyed up. "Let me give you a massage, sweetheart. You're all balled up like a spool of steel wire." Obediently Carly slipped her nightgown over her head and stretched out on her bed, allowing Jesse to knead her flesh with his long, tan fingers. He couldn't help the erection that rose in his jeans as he touched her soft skin and slid his hands down her smooth back to the gentle slope of her bare buttocks only partially covered by the sheets.

When she flipped over and opened her arms to him, her expression was pleading. *Make love to me*, it said. He obeyed, taking her gently at first, as if she was made of fine china. It was Carly who thrust up, pulling him further into her, grabbing his hips and using his body like it was some kind of drug.

When at last they fell apart, they bodies glimmering with sweat, Carly was almost instantly asleep, the horrible tension of the situation broken at last, at least for the moment. Jesse lay next to her in the room lit only by a neon sign outside the small apartment window.

She looked so young, so vulnerable there asleep, her tousled curls framing her rounded cheeks. Jesse felt he could stare at that lovely face forever. When he finally did succumb to sleep himself, her face continued to sweeten his dreams.

* * * * *

Anthony was eager to talk once he realized who Jesse was. They agreed to meet at a small diner not far from the Club de Sade, which had been temporarily closed due to the investigation. "Thank *God*, you're on the case, Jesse! It's been horrible, you have no idea! Carly isn't the only one they've questioned, you know. They spent *hours* grilling me over the same things—was the alarm set, who had a key, who had a reason to harm the victim, did I have a criminal record. Can you *imagine*?"

Jesse started to answer but Anthony wasn't finished. "And with the club closed down, we're all out of a job! We live from client to client, you know. It's our bread and butter! Amanda is fit to be tied, I can tell you! And what I've been through! One of those nasty cops actually frisked me! Frisked me, like I was some kind of common criminal! I was *mortified*!" Jesse didn't think

Anthony looked especially mortified—in fact he seemed rather excited by it all, but Jesse refrained from comment.

"Let's focus, Anthony. The sooner we can get this solved, the sooner Carly's name will be cleared and you can get back to business." As Anthony looked chastened Jesse said apologetically, "I know I'll be rehashing some stuff you've already been over with the cops, but you and I are looking at it from a different perspective perhaps than they do. We want to find information that can help us clear her name, not convict her."

Anthony nodded earnestly and leaned forward. "I understand. Ask me anything. I don't know if I can help, but I sure want to. Carly's such a sweetie. Such an innocent, really."

Jesse nodded and flipped open his notebook. He spent several minutes reviewing the physical layout of the club, how people got in and out, who had keys and access codes and what people's schedules were. He took detailed notes even though nothing was leaping out at him yet. He knew from experience that one little fact, one little discrepancy, was enough to change the slant on something completely or even unravel a whole case.

"Okay, based on your gut, was there anyone inside the club with any reason to want 'Hank' dead? Think about it before you answer. Anyone at all?"

"No one else really knew him, as far as I know. Mistress Marlena, that's Carly, she took over for Mistress Jolene once she skipped town. The only other person who really had any contact was me. Oh, and the receptionist Brittany. But she didn't last long."

Jesse stopped taking notes. He hadn't read anything about a Brittany in the police reports, though admittedly they had been incomplete. "Brittany. Who's that? Where'd she go? When did she go?"

"Oh, she landed some modeling contract. Rushed off after only two weeks on the job. And she was good, too! She knew how to use the computer and keep appointments. She seemed to take a real interest in the clients. She knew who was who and she showed up for work, that's a big plus." Anthony smiled ruefully. "But you know these would-be model-actress types. Got her big break and hit the road. Didn't even give me any notice. Just an apologetic phone call. I was still looking for a new receptionist when all this shit hit the fan. Didn't even give me back the key when she left. The little rat claimed she'd lost it. I had to get a new one made."

Jesse looked up from his notepad. "Didn't give you the key?"

"No," Anthony said, suddenly thoughtful. "I was just annoyed at the time, because it was my only spare copy. She was practically in tears with her apologies. I wasn't really worried from a security standpoint, since she was moving to Chicago for this catalog thing—"

Jesse felt the first real surge of hope in the two days since Carly's tearful phone call from the jail. A new person coming into the club and then disappearing without warning, a missing key, a catalog company. These were little niggling clues—things that didn't fit just right, or things that fit all too well in a puzzle that needed solving. At least he had something to focus on, something the police hadn't seemed to pick up on, something that might save his darling girl.

"Do you think it's important, Jesse? I seriously doubt Brittany would have murdered one of our clients! She was just kid! Actually she was even religious, if you can believe it. At least, she gave a reference for this church guy, though I didn't bother checking it at the time. I felt more comfortable frankly calling the restaurant reference than some church!" He laughed and crossed his leather-clad legs, smoothing his long hair back behind his ears.

"Did you tell the police about this Brittany? What's her full name?"

"Brittany Lane, and no, I didn't. I just answered questions and there were plenty of 'em, believe you me. I've read enough crime novels to know not to volunteer information! One of those guys would have loved to have me volunteer something about the club to get us shut right down! Or me arrested! I could tell, the way he looked at me like I was some kind of pervert! Just because whips and chains turn us on doesn't make us *bad*, does it?"

"Focus, Anthony. Focus. I think we might be onto something here. I want to find out all I can about this Brittany Lane. Do you have her employee file? I want to see that church reference and I want to follow up on that catalog company. Those are two elements that also involved Henry Franklin. And his wife Edna. Perhaps especially his wife," he said, more to himself than Anthony.

"I don't have the files. The cops took everything. *Everything!* Our client names and addresses. Oh! This will ruin us. No one will ever come back, not with cops swarming through their private stuff—"

Jesse held up a hand. "Not now. No offense, but I don't care about your club right now. I care about Carly. Thanks for meeting with me." He stood up and threw a few crumpled bills on the table, which more than covered the cost of his coffee and roll. "I'll keep you posted."

Chapter Eleven

ଊ

Carly seemed to be in reasonably good spirits, given the shock of the murder. Eva had come over at once, calling in sick to work to spend the day with her while Jesse went out to investigate. Having a friend there who knew and loved her made Jesse feel more comfortable about leaving her.

When he came back after meeting with Anthony, Jesse asked, "How're you holding up, Carly?" taking her in his arms and kissing her tenderly. Eva had had to go a little while before to meet her on-again boyfriend, George.

"I'm okay, really. I feel so useless though! I want to get out and interview people myself, find out who did this and get them behind bars!"

Jesse didn't want to discourage Carly's active participation in solving the crime, but at the same he was mindful there was still a real killer at large, someone who had murdered Carly's client and set it up to place the blame on her. He wasn't at all keen on his innocent young lover heading out in the big, bad city by herself, without experience or a way of protecting herself.

He managed to convince her it would be best if she stayed put. He did ask that she devise a chart for him, outlining all the people who had been at the club during the murder, the layout of the old brownstone and any possibly motivations for Franklin's demise. She hadn't come up with much, but the exercise kept her busy and gave Jesse something to work with when he came back to her apartment.

Carly put on a brave face, but when Jesse held her at night, she was restless, sometimes crying out in her sleep. The nightmare of her real life seemed to follow her into the darkness so that her face looked bruised and tired even after a full night's sleep.

Now at least he had something to report—the first real glimmer of hope in the investigation. "Brittany Lane," he said, to Carly's confusion.

Carly looked up, startled. "What? What about her? How do you know her?"

"She was the receptionist, right?"

"Yes, before she quit. Anthony was really irked when she just called up and said she wasn't coming back. But that was before the murder. She wasn't there anymore when it happened."

"I know she wasn't, but I have a feeling about this one, Carly. It just takes one clue, one loose thread, and then you catch a hold of it and you pull, gently, carefully, and watch the whole thing unravel. Nothing's been substantiated yet, but there may be a connection. She gave a church as a reference and she quit the job to go do modeling for a catalog company."

As surprise and interest mingled on Carly's face, he continued, "I called Captain O'Reilly down at the precinct but he had left for the day. First thing tomorrow I'm going to go down there and see her file. We may be onto something."

For a moment Carly's expression lighted with hope. She looked so sweet and vulnerable, so trusting that he could save her. Jesse sat down on the edge of the rumpled bed where she sat, a novel resting open on her belly. Gently he smoothed back some unruly golden curls that had fallen over her forehead. Her big blue eyes were still troubled and Jesse longed to take her mind at least for a moment from the murder.

"Do you still belong to me, Carly Stevens?"

A little sparkle lit her eyes as Carly answered, "Yes, Jesse Hernandez. With all my heart."

"Stand up, give me your hand."

Carly stood, her eyes on Jesse's face. He felt his cock rising as he watched her unbend gracefully, her nipples rising against the soft fabric of her T-shirt. He led her into the bathroom and said, "Have seat, your highness. This evening your master is going to be your slave. I want to bathe you and pamper you." He pointed to the "throne" that is, the toilet seat, and Carly sat down on the lid ginning at him.

She watched as Jesse poured her bath, spilling a sweet-smelling oil into the water that filled the room with its aroma as the steam billowed from the tub.

"I think it's ready," he said finally, turning around toward her in the small bathroom. Holding out his hand to her he said, "Come on, sweetheart. Climb in and see if the temperature's good for you."

Carly obeyed, pulling her little T-shirt over her head and stepping out of her jeans and panties. Jesse had to resist his urge to throw her on the bath rug right then and there, and fuck her silly. That could come later.

Gracefully Carly lifted a foot over the tub to touch the water. Carefully she stepped in, sat down and sank back, a little sigh of pleasure escaping her lips. Carly loved to take long, hot baths. It was a luxury to have a real tub in such a small apartment and one of the reasons Carly had rented the place.

Jesse took a little pitcher Carly kept on the side of the tub for the purpose and filled it with the hot, soapy water. "Close your eyes," he warned as he spilled it over her head. Refilling it twice more, he emptied the pitcher over her until her hair was wet enough to shampoo.

He squeezed a large dollop of a fragrant shampoo into his palm and rubbed his hands together for a moment to warm it before leaning up to rub it into her hair. He reached for a little towel to dry her face, gently patting the delicate cheeks as she lay still, her eyes closed, the circles dark beneath them.

Carly smiled a little smile of sheer pleasure as he began to massage her head in slow, firm circles. Using fresh water, he rinsed her hair until it was squeaky clean. Then he gently soaped her body, lingering at her soft breasts, savoring the heft and sweetness of them. He washed her flat belly and soaped her dark blonde little mound, pressing her legs apart so he could clean her secret places — none of which were secret from him.

He bit his lip to distract himself from his own rising desire. Carly was exquisitely beautiful to him. How he longed to get past the torture and uncertainty of this murder investigation, so they could concentrate on their budding relationship without the pall of this tragedy hanging over them.

"You want to stay in a while longer?" he asked.

"Hmmm," she murmured, sighing happily. "I feel wonderful. I didn't realize my muscles were so tense!" She opened her eyes and said, "Thank you, Jesse. No one's ever done that for me before. It was heavenly. You may have gotten yourself a new job!"

He laughed and added more hot water to the tub so she could soak in peace. He folded a towel behind her wet head to protect her from the cold porcelain. Instead of leaning down to bite those perfect little cherry nipples, he contented himself with memorizing her form and shape as she lay quietly in the tub, her body relaxing at last, the trace of a smile still on her lips.

* * * * *

Jesse flipped open his notebook. "Brittany Lane. That's her name. Have your people followed up on a Brittany Lane?"

"Let's see." Captain O'Reilly pulled a folder from one side of his desk and placed it on a pile of other papers. It was considerably thicker than when he had first slid it across the desk for Jesse to read.

Flipping through the pages he said at last, "I don't see anything. Who is she? What's this about?" O'Reilly knew better than to dismiss Jesse Hernandez out of hand. There had been too many times when Jesse had produced a little clue, a thread of evidence that ended up breaking a case wide open.

Jesse explained the connection, noting the rather odd coincidences of a church and a catalog company. "We need to see her file. Her employee file. Your people took all the Club de Sade's files and hers should be in there. She was only there for a couple weeks. The weeks just prior to Henry Franklin's death. She left only four days before the murder was committed. We need to find out where she is and question her. Now."

O'Reilly picked up a phone and gave some orders. In a few minutes a uniformed officer brought the folder in question. Jesse stood up and came around behind the captain so he could see the file along with him. O'Reilly didn't protest.

"Look for her original application. Wherever she put her references. Let's see the name of that church." O'Reilly sifted through the papers for a moment. Jesse used all his self-control not to rip the folder from O'Reilly's hands to look for himself.

The captain drew a piece of paper out and laid it flat on top of the folder. "Here it is," he said. "Let's see. Brittany Lane, address, education, blah, blah." He ran his finger down the sheet as he spoke. "Ah, here it is. References. Guido Santini—Guido's Italian Restaurant. Reverend Julius Johnson, Metropolitan Tabernacle Church." He looked up at Jesse and said, "Holy shit."

"Bingo. Find out her connection to the church and to the catalog company and I think we'll have ourselves the real killer. I have a feeling the name of that catalog company is going to be the very one our Mr. Franklin worked for. The very one owned by Mrs. Edna Franklin's papa."

Jesse let the police take over. He knew with their manpower and resources they could track down Brittany Lane and find out just what her connection to all this was. Once they had the lead, it was relatively easy to ascertain that Ms. Lane had indeed gone to Chicago for a modeling shoot at the L. J. Smathers & Co. headquarters. A call from the New York City police convinced the human resource department there to share the address and telephone number of their newest clothing model.

"Oh, my God," she breathed when the detective identified himself. "What's happened? Something has happened!" When he told her she was being questioned in connection with the murder of Henry Franklin her shriek almost pierced his eardrum over the phone line.

Once she had calmed down sufficiently, the detective was able to determine not only had Brittany known Mr. Franklin as "Hank", but she knew his wife as well, and a good deal better. Brittany readily admitted to taking the job at Club de Sade at Mrs. Franklin's encouragement.

"Do you think Mrs. Franklin did it?" she said breathily. "You *must* be mistaken. She's a devout, religious woman. Why, it's a sin to commit murder! She just wanted to find out what her sneaky husband was up to behind her back. Mrs. Franklin was just trying to save him from the error of his evil ways! Make him see the light.

"Though to tell you the truth—" she suddenly confided, as if talking to a friend instead of a police officer conducting a murder investigation, "—Hank really was harmless. He had strange tastes, yes, tastes that Mrs. Franklin surely wouldn't have put up with in their home. But he was discreet about it. I learned a lot, really, working at the club. I used to think that sexual deviance stuff was just evil, but I really think it's more kind of pathetic. Lonely even. I mean, we're all God's creatures. Who's to say what is pleasure and what is sin?"

Ignoring this perhaps profound revelation for the young woman, the police detective focused her back to the matter at hand, getting her to recall just when she had noticed her key to the club was missing. "Well, I didn't really notice until I called Anthony to give my notice. That's the manager of the club. He's gay but you know I even think that's okay now—"

Again the detective cut her off. Patiently he questioned Brittany, getting her to remember that she had the key for certain up until the day before she decided to quit. "Well, Mrs. Franklin was pretty adamant. She wanted me out of that den of iniquity, as she called it. She was worried I was getting corrupted she said. And it was so fortunate that her daddy owned this catalog company. My big break, really. I always knew if I could just get a chance—"

A thinly veiled threat on the part of the detective to have Brittany arrested and flown back to New York City under arrest as a material witness focused her again. She thought a while and said, "I must have lost it at church. Either that or on the way home from church. It was on my key ring. I guess it must have fallen off. I quit the club the next day, since Mrs. Franklin helped me to get that modeling contract."

The detective asked a few more questions, noting the direct connection between Mrs. Franklin, Brittany's applying for the job at the club, the key "going missing" at the church when Mrs. Franklin was present and the fact that the older woman managed to get Brittany a modeling contract, which necessitated a move out of state.

"Very close, are you, you and Mrs. Franklin?"

"Well, I guess we are. I mean—" Brittany paused, a note of confusion entering her voice "—we weren't especially close, but I guess she's just a good Christian woman, looking to help out a young person like me." Brittany still seemed oblivious of the implications of the information she had provided the detective. At least she presented herself that way.

As he was hanging up, the cop warned her to remain available and advised her she would almost certainly have to come back to New York to testify in a murder trial. A very shaken Brittany promised she would stay close to the phone.

* * * * *

"The thread, Carly! The case is unraveling! I was right about Brittany. The connection is more than confirmed! It's the break we've been waiting for. It's all falling into place!" Jesse burst into Carly's apartment after his visit to the station, eager to fill her in on the breaking events and their implications.

As he spoke, Carly's eyes brightened with understanding. Jesse tried to contain his own enthusiasm but he was doing a poor job of it. In fact, at one point he grabbed his lover in a big embrace and whirled her around the room. They were both laughing as he dropped down to the couch and let her roll off and settle next to him, nestled against his shoulder.

"But Jesse, this is pretty horrible. You're saying Mrs. Franklin is the prime suspect now! His *wife*, for God's sake! The one woman in the world who should stand by her man and love him through thick and thin! Do you really think *she's* the murderer? And how could she do it? How did she get in there and slit his throat while I was out of the room? It's just too bizarre to imagine!"

"I agree with you. It's horrible to even imagine. Yet I can't help but be glad she's the focus of their investigation now. They're no longer interested in you as the prime suspect. That was my number one concern, and now we've accomplished that. It's hard to focus yet on the specifics of the crime—I'm just so relieved we've given someone a motive and opportunity. Now the police just have to prove the means."

Jesse grinned, relief making him almost weak. The police were hard at work now, their energies now firmly focused on Mrs. Edna Franklin. "Well, it's not over yet. They haven't arrested her. But O'Reilly as much as told me it's only a matter of time. They've brought her in for questioning. There's a team going over the 'blue room' for any DNA evidence that will link the wife to the place."

Carly looked up at her lover. The warmth of her smile seemed to dispel the shadows in the room. "I knew you'd do it. I knew it," she whispered.

* * * * *

Jesse sat in the police captain's office, the folder in his hands. The captain had allowed him to read the final report. A second search of her condo had unearthed the missing key to

Club de Sade, which they had found secreted between the pages of a Bible. After they had taken her down to the station, advising her she was under arrest for the murder of her husband and the right to an attorney, Edna Franklin had broken down, confessing to the murder.

It had been, she claimed, a "crime of passion". Not passion for her husband, she had gone on to explain, but a passion for the Lord. She was doing the Lord's work and she knew in her heart one day she would receive her just reward at the right hand of God.

O'Reilly, pushing his heavy hair off his forehead for the fifth time in as many minutes, commented, "Talk about religious convictions gone awry! That lady is whacko city."

"I don't know," Jesse said, leaning back on two legs of his chair. "In the end I don't think it was about religion. She wasn't out to save his soul, despite what she claims. I think it was more about a woman scorned. A broken, twisted heart." He shook his head and added, "Thank God, you found the real murderer, though. And cleared Carly's name."

"You gave us the clue we needed, Hernandez."

Jesse shook his head dismissively. "Nah, you would have come up with it the next day. I just hurried things along. Lucky break."

"Yep, you're one of the luckiest guys I know," O'Reilly grinned. He'd seen Carly when she was brought into the station for questioning. A buzz had spread around the station that Meg Ryan was being booked for murder.

Back at Carly's place, Jesse recounted what he had read in the Franklin case files. "I think bottom line is Edna just went nuts. Plain crazy. She might get a reduced sentence because she claims she didn't plan to actually *kill* him. Not premeditated. She just wanted to confront him in his 'den of sin' and 'make him see the light'. I'm not sure it'll fly, though. She did a lot of pretty premeditated shit to break and enter into Club de Sade—lining up that receptionist job for Brittany, stealing her key, shipping her off to Chicago once she had the information she was after."

"I wonder how she got in, though. Even with a key, you need the access code."

"She was clever, that Edna. And Brittany, well, let's just say she leaves something to be desired in the brains department. She unwittingly gave Edna the information she needed about the code. Slipped and told her it was the owner's dog's birthday. Four digits. Edna must've tried out the more obvious combinations and struck pay dirt.

"She went in through the kitchen, which apparently isn't used much by the staff." As Carly nodded in confirmation, he continued. "She climbed the back stairs and hid in an empty room, actually the 'red room' where Anthony put you after you passed out. Brittany had told her of your pattern of stepping out mid-session to get a soda."

Carly interjected. "Is there anything she *didn't* tell this woman? Jesus, this is so bizarre!"

"You can say that again. It gets weirder. Edna waited until you were out of the room and down the stairs. Two of the other rooms were occupied, for God's sake. With incredible nerve she slipped into your room and saw her husband in his, uh, glory. She must have acted immediately."

Jesse paused. He didn't want to make Carly relive that horrible moment when she had come in to find the murder victim shackled to the chair, covered in his own blood. Carly, sensing why he had paused whispered, "I see it still. In my dreams. My nightmares." She hugged herself, looking like a small, frightened child.

They were sitting on the little couch that almost filled Carly's tiny living room. Jesse pulled her toward him, taking her in his arms and rocking her slowly. "I know, sweetie, I know. It's so ironic that he died experiencing his ultimate fantasy, right down to a knife at his throat. At least we know it was quick. He probably never knew what hit him. In seconds it was over."

Carly's head was bowed. Jesse lifted her face with his finger under her chin. He couldn't stop the tears that sprang to his own eyes as he saw the ones spilling over her cheeks. He kissed them away, silently thankful that at least now the healing process could begin.

He was ready to change the subject, wanting to protect her, but Carly now seemed eager to hear more. "How did she justify what she did, Jesse? Did she tell them that? How could she possibly claim to love Jesus and be religious, and then go and do the horrible thing she did? Especially her, with her belief in hellfire and damnation? Doesn't she think she's going to burn now herself, for all eternity? Isn't she terrified of the wrath of her particular brand of God?"

"She's crazy, Carly. Logic doesn't apply. But I did read some of the transcript of her confession. She said something about the ends justifying the means. That the Lord would forgive her because he knew she was acting to save Henry's soul. She also said she hadn't meant to kill him, just scare him a little. Scare him 'straight' if you will. To her credit, she did break down and start crying while she was talking about it. The transcript indicates a twenty-minute break while they allowed her to get control of herself."

"Scare him by sticking a knife into his throat?" Carly was incredulous. It just didn't sound right.

"That struck me as odd, too. It looked like a professional job—even the police noted that. But unless they can find evidence that she knew how to slit someone's throat like that, they'll probably go for a lesser charge than first-degree murder. More of a crime of passion."

"Evidence. Like what?"

"Like books in her home about wartime guerilla war methods of assassination perhaps."

"Or on a computer," Carly offered. "They could check the Internet history of websites she's visited."

"Yes. That would be incriminating. But she didn't have a computer at home. I remember the cops wanted to see her emails and files but the Franklins didn't own a computer."

"How about the church? Didn't she spend all her free time there?"

Jesse nodded thoughtfully. "Yes," he said slowly. "You might have a career in detection, Ms. Stevens."

Carly's supposition was confirmed. The police, with Reverend Johnson's permission, took the church computer back to headquarters as potential evidence. It didn't take long to find several sites that had been visited, which were hosted by various nefarious terrorist groups with handy tips on murder by knife, bomb or poison.

Instead of feeling proud or vindicated, Carly found she only felt sickened and sad. Edna Franklin was a deeply disturbed woman who had taken another person's life in cold blood. Carly had been caught in the middle, unwittingly playing a part in a very risky game.

Chapter Twelve

ഊ

The room was packed. Carly stood to the side of the little raised dais in the center, her head bowed, her hands clasped loosely in front of her. She could hear the people murmuring and she knew some of them were talking about her.

"Look at how still she stands. So calm! Can you imagine? If that was me up there just waiting for my turn to be publicly whipped, I'd be fidgeting and about to wet my pants!"

Carly suppressed a little smile. She did have butterflies in her stomach. In fact she marveled that she was standing here at all, dressed only in a sheer golden silk dress that came to mid-calf, with a long sexy slit up each side. It was cut low and closely fitted to reveal her cleavage and was held up by thin straps on her bare shoulders. Her wrists were loosely shackled with fine gold mesh chain, more for show than actual restraint. Beneath the dress, Carly wore only a thong of the same shimmery gold material.

Though she herself was unaware of it, with her peaches and cream coloring offset by the shiny gold dress clinging to her lithe feminine curves, she looked like some kind of wanton angel standing there in her bare feet, with her honey blonde hair falling in unruly curls over her bowed face.

When Jesse had asked her if she'd like to be his "model slave" for his latest demonstration, she had been at once honored and unnerved.

"Me?"

Edna Franklin was safely behind bars awaiting her trial for murder. Jesse and Carly were in his living room, standing together at his large picture window watching the sun set over the Hudson River. Having made love earlier in the afternoon, they were both still scantily dressed—Jesse in silky black boxers and Carly in a pink satin nightgown, which came to the knee.

Jesse had taken her in his arms, drawing her tight against him. She loved the feel of his firm, broad chest against her breasts. She could feel her nipples responding as always and a sweet warmth moistening her sex. "Why not you? Aren't you my lovely submissive girl? It's at a very posh club, that new one in the Village called Whipped. They want a lecture on submissive headspace, on the dynamics of a loving D/s relationship. Of course they want the standard whipping demo. They have a group that meets there once a month. It's a group called Power Exchange. They're all couples, so it's not like some wanker-fest for lonely boys and old men. You won't be ogled. No one will make a pass at you, if that's what you're worried about."

"Oh, it's not that so much," she had replied. "It's the public aspect of it. I've come to adore what you and I share. I love submitting to you sexually. I've never felt so vulnerable and powerful at the same time. But it's something else again to be publicly whipped and displayed!"

Jesse had answered, "Remember Angela? Remember the visceral response you had to watching her on stage?" Carly shivered. She did remember. She remembered the easy sensual grace with which Angela handed the whip to Jesse, then unknown to Carly. The way she had knelt without self-consciousness and allowed first Jesse and then another man to whip her. Carly remembered her own feelings of awe, confusion and arousal as she watched the whipping, not yet tuned in to her own masochistic and submissive yearnings.

Jesse stroked Carly's cheek, drawing his finger down the line of her cheekbone. "You asked me how Angela had submitted like that. Remember how you said she seemed almost rapturous, in a state of bliss? I've seen that in *you*, Carly. When you 'fly' you get like that. Wouldn't it be amazing if we could share that with others? To show other curious D/s couples what is possible? To allow them to see the potential of the sublime? That it goes beyond kinky fun and games?"

Carly was quiet a moment. In a small voice she asked, "Would I have to be naked?"

Jesse laughed and kissed the top of her blonde head. "Only if you wanted to be, sweetheart."

Now here she was, not naked, but dressed in an outfit that clearly defined her firm, high breasts, the nipples taut against the cool silk. She did feel vulnerable, but very sexy as well. Jesse had seemed quite pleased when she said she would do it, and had promised her *she* would be the one in control.

"I'll be the one with the whip, yes. And I'll talk to the audience. But you and I are so in tune. You'll let me know if I'm going too far, or if something doesn't feel right. It's a paid gig, by the way, so you'll take home a few bucks. Not enough to retire, but hey."

Carly had laughed. The money was the least of it. Though she was starting to feel more than a little concerned about how she was going to make a living. Three weeks had passed since Edna Franklin had been arrested for the murder of her husband. Luckily Carly had money saved, but it certainly wouldn't last forever.

The thought of resuming her fledgling career as a Dominatrix repelled her. Though intellectually she knew it wasn't the job itself that had been dangerous and that the murder had nothing directly to do with her, emotionally she knew she could never return to the business. The image of poor Hank, bloodied and naked, bound to the chair, still awoke her in the night, drawing sobs of terror that only receded when Jesse took her in his arms and soothed her back to sleep.

But what else could she do? Her entire career before this little foray had been spent with L. J. Smathers & Co. She knew the business and she loved it, but she'd quit in a huff and it seemed unlikely they'd rehire her, even if she came crawling back willing to take a pay cut. And she wasn't sure her pride would permit it. Still, there were other clothing catalogs in the world…

Focus, Stevens, she admonished herself. Again the shadow of a smile touched her mouth. If only those tittering women behind her knew she wasn't standing there in chains reflecting on her status as "slave girl", but was actually thinking about how to pay the rent!

As the lights dimmed, her thoughts were jerked back to the present in a hurry. The room wasn't large—it held maybe twenty small tables, all of which were filled with men and women, mostly in street clothes, but some were in leather or dressed even more scantily than Carly. This was "the scene" and Carly was no longer surprised. She'd lost her wide-eyed wonder at how casually these people would strip when "ordered" by their "masters". Wasn't she now standing in a submissive pose awaiting her dominant lover's bidding?

Two stage lights were focused on the dais. Carly, still standing just below it and to the side, was partially obscured in the shadows. Yet all eyes were upon her. Her mouth felt dry and yet it was exciting to be standing there in her sexy golden dress, the focal point of attention for all the people gathered at the club that evening. When Jesse emerged from a side door, she couldn't help but steal a glance at her lover.

He looked gorgeous in the white linen shirt she had helped him to buy, simply tailored and cut to show his broad shoulders and chest to perfection. His tan leather pants looked like toffee poured over his sexy ass and strong, long legs. His "package" was exquisitely pouched in the soft leather and she actually felt her mouth water as he brushed by her, all male and sexy as hell.

Carly felt a catch in her throat. It was still hard for her to believe that this handsome, sexy man was actually in love with her. And she with him.

"Good evening, ladies and gentlemen, Doms and subs. My name is Jesse Hernandez and I have been given a very special privilege tonight. I've done a number of these demonstrations over the years. In fact, I see some familiar faces here tonight."

There was a smattering of applause as he continued. "But I've never had the honor of sharing my own submissive's grace and charm for your pleasure."

Jesse who was standing on the dais, gestured toward Carly. She stood still, hoping no one could see her knees were trembling. It wasn't so much that she was embarrassed to be standing there being scrutinized by the audience, it was the fear she would make a fool of herself during this very public display.

She knew Jesse was hoping she would "fly". Thankfully she also knew he understood it wasn't something she could control or direct. It just happened, or it didn't. She had "flown" a number of times in the privacy of his apartment, experiencing the intense euphoria and deep erotic calm that came after an extended session. It wasn't something she could control or bring on at will.

How would she react in front of a bunch of strangers? She secretly doubted she would be able to relax enough to really get into the moment, but no matter what happened, she wanted to behave with grace and not let her lover down.

Jesse spoke for about fifteen minutes, lecturing on his favorite subject, the romance of erotic submission, and taking questions as they came up. He talked in general terms about the need of a Dom to respect and cherish his or her sub, never assuming they should take whatever was meted out "because they were submissive". It was always, he reminded the D/s couples there, "a matter of trust". He talked about how much more intense the experience could become when love entered the equation. He smiled tenderly at Carly as he said a Dom must never betray the gift of submission given by their sub.

As he spoke Carly kept her head down, remembering how Angela had stood in just this position, stock-still and patient as a stone. But she saw her lover in her mind's eye, taking her to the edge of pleasure, guiding her through erotic pain to emerge into something stronger than either sensation, something wild and free that made her feel as if life had only just started at that moment and all the world was ripe and new.

"Carly." His smooth baritone sliced through her reverie. She looked up and Jesse was holding his hand out to her. Slowly Carly climbed the three little stairs that brought her next to him on the little stage. She was thankful she was barefoot—at least she had no heels to totter on.

She stood next to Jesse, facing the audience, her wrists still prettily bound in front of her. He had told her all she had to do was stand still and face the audience when he called her up. He would direct her after that.

"Carly has agreed to submit to a sensual whipping while you watch. This isn't just to turn you on or show you what she can take. If you're all quiet and focus with us, Carly may be able to 'fly' while you watch. As I touched on earlier, it's a kind of trance state that can be induced during an intense physical session. For Carly this can happen when she's being whipped with our heavy suede flogger. I won't make any promises—those of you who have played publicly know you can't just will this sort of thing. It has to come of its own accord or not at all.

"Either way, I'm sure you'll enjoy watching this stunning woman submit to the kiss of my lash. And for those of you new to the whip, pay attention to my stroke, to my hand position and grip. It's all in the wrist." Smiling, he turned toward Carly and stroked her cheek, looking deep into her blue eyes with his dark chocolate ones. She stared back and the room seemed to fall away. He was all there was at that moment.

He murmured for her ears only, "You are beauty incarnate. You make my heart ache you're so lovely. Thank you for this. I know I'll be proud of you. I already am." Gently he pressed her shoulder, causing Carly to sink gracefully to the floor of the little stage, which was carpeted with a soft, thick rug.

She was facing the audience who were now completely silent, riveted to the scene before them. "Raise your arms," Jesse said in a normal tone so the audience could hear. Carly obeyed, the long chain wrapped around her wrists glittering in the stage light.

Jesse stood to the side of his charge. Bending down, he caressed her right breast, circling it until his fingers found the nipple, which he lightly pinched. Carly gasped slightly, not expecting to be touched like this in front of them all. It was a gesture of ownership and it served its purpose, making Carly at once nervous and aroused, underscoring her position there on the stage as Jesse's slave girl.

She was kneeling back on her haunches, her legs pressed tightly together. "Open your knees as wide as you can," he ordered quietly. She looked up at him pleadingly but his expression was firm. Taking a deep breath she did as he commanded, so the audience had a view of her crotch, though it was covered in the golden silk of her thong. She understood this was yet another gesture on her part of her submission to him. She was willing to bare herself as he commanded. She knew he would go no further, as she had told him beforehand that she didn't want to be naked in front of the audience and he had promised to respect her wishes.

It was as if the audience was holding its collective breath. Jesse walked behind the young woman and picked up the whip he had been discussing earlier in his presentation. It was the same heavy, braided flogger he had used on Angela in what seemed a lifetime ago.

Carly knelt in position, knees parted, back straight, her arms still raised over her head. Jesse said, "Assume the position. Hands behind your head." She obeyed, locking her fingers behind her neck. Slowly he dragged the whip across Carly's back. She took another breath, willing herself to be calm.

At first the lash was soft, smoothing her bare shoulders and back, sliding across the silk of her dress. It felt good. Thuddy and sexy—no sting yet. That would come, she knew.

Jesse guided her skillfully, always waiting until the very moment when *she* was the one who wanted more. *Do it harder*, she whispered in her head, not daring to voice her need aloud on that little stage. But he knew, he could feel it in her movements, in her little sighs and moans. She was ready for more.

Soon his strokes came more in earnest, a real whipping now. She felt the sting of all those little braided strips of leather slapping at her skin and through the silk that protected her not at all. She felt the pain and yet her brain didn't interpret it as something negative. Her body interpreted it as something good, making her pussy wet and swollen.

Carly's eyes had fluttered shut and her mouth was open — lips parted. Her tongue was running itself along her lower lip as she moaned softly, oblivious now of the people sitting at their tables enjoying her as their evening's entertainment.

She wanted more! More! She opened her eyes and turned back toward Jesse who lowered his whip hand and leaned down. "What, sweetheart?" he whispered. "You're doing beautifully. You were born for this."

"More," she begged. "I need more. I need to stand up." He understood. She had always been standing when she "flew" in the past.

Unclasping the gold chain that was still wrapped around her wrists, he pulled it free and let it fall to the ground. Carly slowly lowered her arms, dropping her hands into her lap. When he offered a hand, she took it, letting him pull her up. Drawing her toward himself, he caught her in a quick embrace and whispered into her hair, "I love you," before turning her so her face was to the audience.

Again he began his dance of dominance, moving around behind her from side to side, the whip catching her back, her ass, her thighs. Occasionally it wrapped around her slim torso, the tips catching her breast or belly and making her cry out.

As he hit her harder, gauging by her reaction that she was ready, she began to shift and shuffle, emitting little whimpering sounds. "No," she moaned, "No, it's too much. I can't, I can't...please..." He didn't stop. He was sweating, his dark hair curling round his ears, his expression intense, even fierce.

And because he didn't stop, because he continued to whip her hard now, as hard as he ever had before, it started to happen. In spite of the audience, in spite of the silk dress, which partially interfered with the lash, in spite of Carly's apprehensions she wouldn't be able to relax enough in front of others, she felt it begin.

As during the other times, the first thing to change was her perception of the pain. She still felt the sting, but it no longer hurt her. It was like a thousand perfect kisses brushing her flesh. The whimpers died out and her wildly pounding heart slowed and then slowed some more. Her head felt heavy, so heavy, and so she let it fall back. She felt her mouth open but didn't have the energy or desire to close it.

She felt like a statue. Or more accurately like a human made of flesh and blood, but encased inside a statue that was lined with the softest bedding, warm and safe. She stood perfectly still, *grace personified*, Jesse would have said.

Joy welled up in her like a bubbling fountain and still he continued to whip her, the only sound in the room the lashes whooshing and falling against tender flesh.

And then it was over. She was aware he had put down the whip but she didn't move, rooted to the spot, her cells flooded with endorphins, her mind at peace, her body on fire with lust. She felt Jesse's arms around her, pulling her gently back to reality.

She became aware of a sound. A smacking, rhythmic sound. The sound of applause. "That's for you," Jesse whispered. "All for you, my darling wonderful girl."

* * * * *

Spring was hinting at its impending arrival, though probably one more winter storm still waited in the wings. It was mid-March and the dogwood trees in Washington Square had tiny pale green buds sprouting along their branches. Soon they would be in full flower, white and pink, dropping their petals on the paths of the park before summer took hold and dark green leaves took their place.

Jesse and Carly were strolling together in the Square one lazy Sunday afternoon when Carly's cell phone rang.

"Hello?" She was quiet for a moment as someone spoke on the other end. They were near a bench and Carly sank down on it. Jesse sat with her, watching her with concern as her eyes widened and she turned toward him, her expression becoming one of surprise.

"I'll have to see," she answered coolly, sounding very dignified and reserved. "I have to tell you, I have several options lined up at the moment." She paused as she listened and then said, "Yes, that would be fine. I can be there on Thursday. Shall we say 10:00? Very good. Thank you. Goodbye."

As she flipped her phone shut, she gave a little whoop and squealed, "Oh, my God! I can't believe it!"

"What? What was that all about? You sounded like somebody's mother or the headmistress of a school. Who *was* that?"

"Oh, just the chief financial officer of L. J. Smathers & Co. calling from Chicago to see if I might be interested in considering a position with the firm. As manager of the clothing line here in New York City!" Her voice rose in an excited squeal.

"You'd consider it? After what they put you through?"

"The *they* in question was Henry Franklin." She paused a moment. Hank was dead. But even though he had been brutally murdered, the fact did remain that professionally he had treated her badly, taking her ideas and keeping her down.

"He's gone now. The position they want me to take is the one I was passed over for last year so they could bring *him* in! Now they're crawling back to *me*! I can write my own ticket!"

She twirled into the grass next to the path, clearly elated at the strange turn of events. Jesse watched her, his expression bemused. She turned back to him, smiling hugely. He said, "I guess you really miss it, huh? You rarely talk about it, but I can see it really matters to you."

"More than you know. That was my life. I had fun until the murder with the whole Dominatrix thing, but I knew I wasn't going to do it forever. It was just a weird sidestep while I got my head on straight, I guess. I was already thinking about getting back into the catalog business. It's what I do. But I never dreamed I'd get this kind of chance. I have so many ideas!"

"But you didn't say yes, did you? Only that you'd go in and hear what they had to say."

"Well, sure. Can't be seen as too eager. I've learned a thing or two over the years, I guess. No more naïve little girl assuming everyone has good intentions and my best interests at heart. They're going to have to pay me *at least* what Franklin was making, which would be double what I was making before I left. And I want carte blanche to implement my ideas, pending management approval, of course."

Jesse laughed and caught Carly up in his arms. "You are amazing," he said before he leaned down to kiss her. "I'm so proud to be in your life. Now let's get home. I need to make love to you until you beg me to stop."

Jesse started speaking suddenly in the deep bass voice of Peter whom they had often joked about since that first night when they met. Peter had voiced his opinion about subs having to submit just because they were submissive and now Jesse teased, "You're my slave — you have to."

Carly grinned and said, "Yes, sir. Right away, sir. As soon as you can catch me."

She took off across the park, surprise giving her the advantage. When Jesse finally caught up to her, they fell together on the new grass, laughing and kissing like playful kittens.

After a time they sobered, lying still under the warm sun, the promise of a life together as new as the buds on the trees. No matter if one was Dom and the other sub, no matter who conceded what sexual power to whom, in the end, it came down to a very simple thing. Love.

About the Author

ɞ

Claire Thompson has written numerous novels and short stories, all exploring aspects of Dominance & submission. Ms. Thompson's gentler novels seek not only to tell a story, but to come to grips with, and ultimately exalt in the true beauty and spirituality of a loving exchange of power. Her darker works press the envelope of what is erotic and what can be a sometimes dangerous slide into the world of sadomasochism. She writes about the timeless themes of sexuality and romance, with twists and curves to examine the 'darker' side of the human psyche. Ultimately Claire's work deals with the human condition, and our constant search for love and intensity of experience.

Claire welcomes mail from readers. You can write to her c/o Ellora's Cave Publishing at 1056 Home Avenue, Akron, OH 44310-3502.

Enjoy An Excerpt From:

Slave Castle

Copyright © Claire Thompson, 2003.

All Rights Reserved, Ellora's Cave, Inc.

Chapter 1

"No! I won't do it!" Marissa's lip trembled, but she stared defiantly at Tom. "You can't make me!"

"I don't want to make you," Tom said quietly, his voice rigid with self-control. Marissa was naked, kneeling on her knees in front of him. Her arms were wrapped around her torso in a protective gesture and her eyes were flashing. Tom sighed. Things weren't working out with Marissa, which was a shame, because he had to admit that he was enormously attracted to her, and desperately wanted to own her.

Looking down on the impossible, gorgeous creature at his feet, he sighed. Marissa's hair was thick and loosely waved, copper-colored in the flickering light of the many candles lit about the spacious master bathroom of Tom's penthouse. It was that hair that first attracted him at the party. It wasn't auburn exactly, and certainly not red. No, if it had to be defined, it was copper, burnished with gold and lustrously tousled now. Her skin was smooth and soft, and her eyes were large and dark as she glared up at him, daring him with her expression.

When she *wanted* to submit, when he 'ordered' her to do what suited her, Marissa could be very submissive, or at least compliant. When he shackled her facedown to a whipping board, legs lewdly splayed on either side, pussy spread against the leather-covered wood, so he could whip her with his new heavy-tressed whip, she obeyed without hesitation. And her moans and cries were so sexy as each blow from the whip forced her little pussy against the leather, the lovely sting of the whip mingling so deliciously with the mounting friction against her clit.

When he ordered her to kneel before him, naked, and hold perfectly still with her mouth open like a little birds, she did so, her eyes sparkling with anticipation. She was like a statue of a goddess as he fucked her face, impaling her so that he knew she couldn't breathe until he pulled back enough to allow it.

But now, as he demanded something that she didn't already want to do, something that would actually require *submission* and not just the satisfaction of her masochistic and sluttish nature, she balked. As with each other task or idea he devised that didn't meet specifically with her own desires, she had resisted, and then refused him. When he had wanted to fuck her ass, Marissa had demurred, telling him she never 'allowed' a man 'back there.'

At first he had been challenged, and he had gotten a thrill from holding her down and 'forcing' her. He had taken her virgin ass, and she had cried out and struggled, but she had orgasmed, screaming his name, and he had realized pretty quickly that what she was after was the fight. She *wanted* him to present suggestions and ideas that she would refuse, so that he could then 'force' her to obey.

And it had been fun, at first. What a wild two weeks they had had since that first night he had brought her home. They had barely left the house, so focused on exploring each other that their bodies were raw from the passion, literally sore to the touch, and yet still the flame seemed to burn in him for her.

He still experienced a delirium of desire when their bodies came together, and he could feel her sweat-slick breasts and belly flattened beneath him. It was as if a bolt of electric current ran through both their bodies, and would only release them from each other when it ceased, leaving long shuddering waves of pleasure in its wake.

They had met at his friend George's house, where she had assured him that she was submissive and wanted, no, was longing for, a 'real' master to take her in hand. She had come with a group of girlfriends, but she had left with him. Against his own better judgement, Tom had taken her home that very night. What ensued could barely be classified as a Dominant/submissive love affair. From the beginning it was more of a fight, with him demanding obedience, and her refusing, or daring him to 'make her', which he would usually do, subduing her through sheer force. It had been exhilarating, leading to wild and clashing sexual encounters that left them both completely spent.

In a word, it was fun, but it wasn't what Tom was seeking. It was a game, and clearly that was what this mysterious young woman was interested in. A game of cat and mouse, where the mouse was completely in control.

Tom, on the other hand, wanted a truly submissive sexual slave who would obey his every command and comply with his every whim, however outrageous. Someone who would kiss the whip after he used it to flog her, someone who would live for the chance to serve him and ache for his tender words.

Somehow Marissa had burned her way under his skin in a way that was very rare for Tom, who liked to think of himself as surrounded by an invisible sheet of ice that kept others at a proper distance. How had she slipped under the ice? When he'd met her at the party, he had been ready to leave. Normally Tom was aloof at these events. His friend George held them several times a year at his country estate in Orange County. The guests were discreetly served by a household of slave girls and boys who saw to everyone's comfort, and also served as the evening's entertainment, if the guests weren't sufficiently titillated with each other.

Tom casually enjoyed the parties, the freely flowing fine champagne and the buffets piled with gourmet foods. The naked and semi-naked servants silently glided about the rooms, serving food and graciously submitting to the gentle and not so gentle fondling by the guests. He would usually pick a slave girl or two and take them off to an adjoining bedroom for a little rough play and sex. But it meant nothing to him. He wouldn't ask their names, and he rarely thought of them again afterwards. It was just a diversion, a relaxation after a hard week investing the money of certain wealthy New Yorkers, which was what Tom did for a living, a very lucrative one.

Now on this late spring afternoon, Tom sat on his balcony overlooking the city. He was nursing a gin and tonic, a rueful smile playing on his face. Marissa was still asleep in his big king-sized bed, sprawled naked across the satin sheets. After their second day together, she had essentially moved in and at the time, Tom hadn't minded. She didn't seem to have a job, and told him she was 'between careers.' She didn't elaborate and he hadn't pressed. For the moment it had been enough to have this nymphomaniac angel slut in his bed.

Now he was growing restless. At 34, he found himself longing more and more often for something more than the one night stands, or the two week stand that this little adventure had so far turned into. Marissa wasn't his dream girl, at least she didn't behave like his dream girl, his slave girl, his submissive angel. He didn't want a little hellcat, however beautiful and erotic. This wasn't going to work, he could see that. Why postpone the inevitable?

He would tell her. He would tell her now.

"Marissa!" Tom called through the screen that separated him from his bedroom. No response. "Marissa! Wake up. Come out here. I need to talk to you."

"You come in here," came her sleepy mumble.

"No. I want you out here. Now." Something in his tone must have made it clear he meant business, because a moment later a sleep tousled and naked Marissa came sauntering out, pushing her hair from her face, totally relaxed in her nudity.

"What, baby?" Her voice was pleasingly low, still husky from sleep.

"I've been thinking, Marissa," Tom leaned back in his chair, shading his eyes as he looked up into Marissa's lovely face. The sun was behind her and he couldn't see her features. "Sit down," he said abruptly. She sat across from him on an overstuffed rattan patio chair, crossing her long bare legs.

"What have you been thinking, Master Sir?" This was Marissa's nickname for Tom. At first he had liked it, thinking she meant it as a term of respect. It had become clear though that this was her private joke. She was her own master, no question of that.

He pursed his lips a moment, wondering how blunt to be, and decided to hell with it. "That it's time for you to leave. It's been really fun, Marissa, but we both should be getting on with our lives now."

Marissa stared at Tom for a second, and then threw her head back, her laugh full throated and deep. "You silly," she said. When he didn't join in her laughter, but merely regarded her impassively, Marissa's laugh faltered and faded altogether. She paled and her large dark eyes seemed to grow even larger.

"But Tom," she began, her voice higher pitched than normal in her distress, "Why? We're so good together. Please! You're kidding, right? Say you're kidding." Her eyes pooled with unshed tears and she knelt in front of him, wrapping her arms around his waist. Her bare breasts pressed sweetly against his knees.

Despite himself, Tom felt his body respond to her touch. Something about her electrified him; he couldn't deny it. But she wasn't for him; he knew this with certainty. She wasn't what he had dreamed of. He steeled himself against her touch and pried her fingers loose, forcing her to let go of him.

Marissa hugged herself, still kneeling naked in front of him. "What did I do, Tom? Did I offend you somehow? Please tell me. Let me fix it! I'll do anything. Anything to stay."

Please, I love you.

She didn't say that, and Tom realized suddenly that it was what he was longing to hear, what might have weakened his resolve and have made him want to keep trying with her. But she didn't say it. She had never said it, though to be fair, neither had he.

Sure she wanted to stay; who wouldn't? She lived in a cramped apartment on Broadway with three roommates. She had no job and no steady lover. Why wouldn't she want to stay in Tom's penthouse overlooking Central Park where a maid cleaned every morning and a cook made their meals when they didn't dine out?

Tom knew that part of his charm, indeed perhaps most it, was due to his wealth. His looks were nothing to speak of, certainly not in his own mind. About 5' 10", Tom had a narrow build, slim with long lean muscles and narrow hips. Glasses usually hid his rather beautiful brown eyes, and his dark hair was thick but fine, falling in a straight fringe that frequently got in his eyes. He didn't have a problem dating women, but he was never sure if they were attracted to him or to his money, and this only added layers to the ice he kept around his heart. Tom stared at her, none of these thoughts articulated, until Marissa began to cry quietly, pretty little tears that welled over dark eyes onto smooth cheeks. Her tears tore at him, but Tom wasn't to be so easily manipulated. Abruptly he stood up. "Listen, I need to clear my head. You can stay here till I get back. We'll talk some more then. I'm sorry, I just can't do this anymore. It's a game for you, but I need more." He left her, still kneeling naked, 30 stories above the teeming city, her head buried in her arms.

Tom didn't go far. One block over and two blocks down, in a small, undistinguished brownstone nestled between large glass buildings was a discreet private club which sported the small sign over its locked doors that said simply, "The Club." Again, it was his friend George McBride who had invited him to join this exclusive group of self-professed dominants who lived or worked in the city and came here to unwind in traditional and less than traditional ways. The Club had the usual bar and tables for casual relaxation and conversation. But it also had a fully equipped dungeon, available by appointment for Doms and their submissives to explore their lifestyle in private, or public, as they chose.

As luck would have it, George was there now, sitting alone at a table, sipping a Bloody Mary and watching a football game on the wide screen TV that covered most of one wall. He gestured a greeting as Tom stood at the entrance of the club, his eyes adjusting to the dim light. Responding to George's unspoken invitation, he joined his friend, sliding into an empty seat as a waitress appeared to take his order.

Small talk was exchanged, though Tom couldn't have told you a minute later what either of them had said. A gin and tonic appeared, smelling sweetly of fresh lime. He took a long drink before leaning back in his chair, staring moodily at the game on TV, seeing nothing.

"So what's up, Tommy?" George asked, his voice hearty and a little too loud in the intimate atmosphere. "You seem kinda bummed. Your newest toy break or something?" He laughed and winked but Tom didn't smile back.

"I guess you could say that," he said, the image of Marissa's tear-stained face crushing his heart like a vice.

"You're talking about the girl with the hair, right? The one you left the party with? That was your first mistake, old boy. Taking her home without checking her out first. Dangerous to think with your cock, though in her case I can't say I blame you!" George laughed suggestively. "She crashed my party, you know. I found out later she didn't have an invitation, but with a bod like that, who cares, right?" Again the wink and the insinuating grin, which normally wouldn't have bothered Tom at all, but for some reason, today irritated him.

George plowed on, "So what happened? Did she find someone better? Or did you? Or are you just tired of that particular piece of ass and coming 'round here for a new one?" George laughed, his expression a leer of implied complicity.

Tom sighed, passing a hand over his forehead, pushing his hair back, though it immediately fell forward again. He was barely paying attention to George, but needed the chance to say aloud what had been torturing his mind for these several days now.

"Her name is Marissa, and no, I'm not tired of her, at least not physically. It's something else. I need more. I'm not so young anymore." He broke off as George started to protest.

George was a good five years older than Tom and still behaved like a teenager, with no intention of 'settling down' in his game plan.

"No, please, George, you know what I mean. I want more. I want a soul mate. I'm tired of this casual sex and the loneliness the next morning, wondering who the person next to me is, and what they're doing there. I need a connection. I need a lover, someone who fits my groove, who is submissive to my dominant will. Who not only understands what I need, but longs to give it. Lives to give it."

He stopped talking, realizing it was hopeless, foolish even, to share these deep feelings with George. George was the consummate party animal. And as Tom should have expected, he laughed derisively and said, "Tommy, Tommy, always the romantic. When will you ever learn? There's no such thing as a 'true submissive.' Your so-called slave girls only exist in erotica novels and porn movies. In real life there's just sluts looking for a good time. They all just want to get off in an exciting new way. And they want to do it in style, which we give them in spades, don't we, Tommy boy? In spades."

Tom looked at George, at his heavy face twisted in a conspiring grimace, the fleshy cheeks that would soon be sliding into jowls, the small pale eyes, close on either side of his smallish upturned nose. There was high color in George's cheeks and Tommy realized he had probably had quite a few Bloody Marys before Tom had joined him. He recognized suddenly that he really didn't like George that much.

They had a long history together, having started out as roommates in graduate school, both hot to get their MBAs and make a killing in the financial markets, which both of them had done, with a vengeance. And while they shared a penchant for submissive women, and whips and chains, that was really where their connection ended.

Tom retreated at that moment, inwardly angry with himself for having divulged his own pain to another man. He changed the subject to George, which was easy to do, as George's favorite topic was George. "Forget all that stuff. I'm just tired," Tom said, forcing his voice to a lightness he did not feel. "Tell me about you. What're you doing here today?"

"Thought you'd never ask. I'm meeting two hot little numbers in a few minutes, down in the dungeon. One is a professional dominatrix, and she's bringing me a new toy. A highly-trained submissive slave girl who I'm gonna pay good money to play with and abuse. She takes a good beating, I'm told. I can beat her till she bleeds if I want to. Of course I'm paying her Mistress, not her. She's the object, I plan to be the subject." He grinned, obviously pleased with his clever turn of phrase.

Tom answered, "A submissive, huh? But you have to 'buy' her, so it's just a game."

"So what? It's all just a game to me. You know that. I know, I know," George put up his hand defensively, "For you it's 'real' – a 'way of life.' You want a 'relationship' with someone who will completely subjugate her will to yours. Well, good luck, buddy. I think that's just fairytale stuff, personally, but whatever floats your boat."

Tom said nothing, refusing to engage in this discussion, but silently wondering if maybe George was right, and his expectations were ridiculous. They watched the game on TV for a while, and then George waved over the waitress, settled his tab and said, "Well, Tommy, I'm off to have some serious fun. My girls are waiting for me." Tom watched his friend, a large man whose substantial muscle was just beginning to turn to fat, lumber toward the back exit that led down to the dungeon.

Tom sipped his drink, holding the cold glass between his palms, thinking of Marissa, and his own foolish dreams. He started when someone said, "Excuse me, but may I join you?" Looking up, Tom saw a slim, rather short man with dark hair, cut short, and a pleasant face, nose a trifle prominent, eyes kind and smiling.

Tom gestured toward the empty seat, curious as to who this person was. He hadn't seen him here before, which surprised him, as the clientele was select and rather small, membership fees naturally excluding most from its ranks.

"Thank you," the man said, and Tom observed a very slight accent, more noticeable as very precise pronunciation than as an actual, identifiable accent. It was slightly British in pronunciation.

"Allow me to introduce myself. My name is André Renaud." He stuck out his hand and Tom automatically took it, noting the firm grip.

"Tom Reed."

"A pleasure, Mr. Reed," André said, as he slipped gracefully into the offered seat. "I couldn't help overhearing a little bit of your conversation with your friend. Please forgive me if I am overstepping, but as we are all of a like mind here," he gestured vaguely around the room, clearly suggesting that they were all 'Doms' here, and rich ones at that. Tom noticed now the fine cut of the man's suit, and the emerald cuff links that were no doubt real.

"Not at all," he answered, wondering what was coming, assuming it had to do with money, as most things did.

"I do not mean to intrude, but I did hear what you were saying. About the longing for a connection, something real with a truly submissive woman." Tom colored slightly, embarrassed to have been overhead in such a vulnerable moment.

The man went on, "I only trouble you because I have the same feelings; the same desires, and know how difficult it is to make such a connection. Very few people are 'true submissives' as you say. Very few are born to it, but it is my humble opinion that they can be 'made.'"

Tom looked at him, confused. "I don't follow you."

"I mean that they can be taught. If a person, man or woman, has certain submissive tendencies, they can be taught to submit in a way that is pleasing and proper. Even if they have already exhibited clearly submissive behaviors, these behaviors can be refined and enhanced with proper training. On the other hand, if they are willful types, brats, I call them, who like a good fight and to be overpowered, they can be instructed in the art of submissive behavior. And in time, they come to actually incorporate that submissiveness into their natures. A good slave can be made, Mr. Reed." He sat back, clearly expecting a response.

"That's interesting. I'm not really sure what you're getting at, though, to tell you the truth." What was the man selling? Tom had a nose for salesmen, and this was one, however refined and elegant he appeared.

"Forgive me, I am not being clear. Specifically, I run a little business." Ah, now for the pitch. "I prefer to think of it as a calling, really. A vocation. I have a small estate near Westchester that I've turned into something which might be of interest to a man of your tastes. A man looking for a 'true submissive' as I believe you said."

Tom pursed his lips, waiting for an offer to use this fellow's escort service, no doubt for a hefty fee. Though already skeptical and ready to dismiss the man, he listened politely, despite the caution bells in his head, as André elaborated.

"My little dream became a reality a number of years ago. I run a little establishment called Chateau L'Esclave."

"Slave Castle," Tom interjected, having minored in French in college.

"Indeed," André nodded, a smile of approval on his face. "It is a very select establishment set up for the training of slaves of the highest caliber. Most of the slaves there already belong to a master or mistress, and have been sent to us to hone their submissive skills. We accept slaves anywhere from a week to a year, depending on their master's particular needs and desires. Slaves are trained in all of the submissive arts, up to the highest standards developed here and in Europe by some of the most prominent and successful trainers in the business. And, of course, we work closely with the master to make sure their needs and desires are incorporated in the training."

Tom wasn't aware there was such a 'business' but he refrained from comment, further intrigued despite himself. "We also have slaves for sale. That is, they have a contract which can be purchased. The sales price and contract terms are negotiated with all parties, including the slave of course. In fact, most of the monies go to the slave, with Chateau L'Esclave naturally taking a fee.

"The slave is part of the negotiations, of course, since though they are completely submissive and 'owned' by their master or mistress, said ownership is completely voluntary. I suppose you could say the slavery is really a 'fiction,' since slavery on its face is illegal. But it becomes very real indeed, with the exchange of power nonetheless binding, despite it being consensual. "We also have a permanent staff of trained slaves, who serve the house with complete subservience. I say permanent, in that they live there, but of course in fact they are free to go."

Tom interjected, "Wait a minute. Let me get this straight. You're saying you own this *slave castle*? A place where real people live 'the life' 24/7? Where people send their girlfriends and wives for a little slave training?! Is this legal? Is this for real?"

"Completely legal and absolutely real." André smiled, sensing he had caught Reed's interest at last. He sat back, lacing his hands over his slim stomach. "It is all voluntary, no one is there against their will. I have an excellent attorney who has meticulously researched our options, and prepared contracts and disclaimers that fully protect all parties."

Tom's mind was racing, turning naturally to Marissa. Would she consent to such 'training'? Would it make a difference? He had to know more. Anticipating his concerns André said, "If this seems like something you might be interested in exploring, I would be delighted to set up a personal tour. I suggest only you coming first. If you have someone in mind that could use a little training, we would bring her along later.

"She would, of course, have to be totally comfortable with the program. It would never work otherwise. We have an excellent program for the 'brats.' You would be amazed at the change we can effect with the right, ah, incentives." He smiled, his eyes twinkling.

"And certainly, as I mentioned, we have slaves 'for sale.' Right now I have two very promising submissive young women who need placement. You could look them over, if you like, as well."

Tom started, suddenly entertaining the possibility of a slave for purchase. The stuff of fantasies, surely, and yet here was this dapper man, calmly informing Tom of his options in the slave market! He felt a little disloyal stab as he thought of Marissa, whom he'd left at home crying, waiting for his ultimatum to allow her to stay or force her to go.

Never a man to give away his intentions, Tom was noncommittal as he accepted Renaud's card. "I'll give you a call," he promised, now eager to get home to Marissa and at least float the idea with her. He realized the little flare of hope that had surged up in him was an indication that Marissa meant more to him than he had been willing to admit. He had to have her, but on his terms. Pocketing the little business card, he took his leave.

Back at the apartment Marissa was waiting, dressed now in a little sundress that made it clear nothing was underneath. Her nipples poked sweetly against the soft fabric, her breasts raised by her arms crossed protectively under them. Her copper hair tumbled around a face bare of makeup, with eyes reddened from crying. She sat curled in one of his large leather chairs, looking like a lost little waif.

"Marissa," the word was wrenched from his lips as he crossed quickly over to her, kneeling at her feet, dropping his head into her lap, "I'm sorry, honey. I'm sorry. I didn't want to make you cry. I just can't keep on how we're going. I don't want the games anymore. I need more."

"What do you want, Tom? Tell me what you want? I'll do it. I'll do anything." Tom felt her cool fingers smoothing the hair from his forehead.

"I want something I'm not sure you can give. And it isn't fair for me to ask it. I want a submissive slave girl. Not a willful sex kitten, I'm sorry. You are incredibly sexy and fun, but it isn't what I want in my life right now."

"Oh, Tom! I can change! I swear I can. I can be what you want! I want to be what you want. I want to be with you." Her voice was pleading, almost a whine.

Until that day, he would have rejected her promise outright. He didn't believe you could 'make a slave' as Mr. Renaud had staunchly affirmed. He believed it was your orientation, plain and simple, and while a slave could be 'trained', they could not be molded into something they were not. And yet here was his darling Marissa, so beautiful and vulnerable, pleading to keep a place in his life. Who was he to make the decree that she couldn't try?

And so, ignoring the little voice inside of himself that said it would never work, he decided to take a chance. Producing the little business card from his pocket, he silently handed it to Marissa.

"What's this?" she asked, taking it. "Chateau L'Esclave – by appointment only," she read. "What's that? Some kind of castle, right? Why are you showing me this? Is it a restaurant?" And so Tom explained about his meeting with the Frenchman, and about this supposed slave castle where they could take someone like Marissa and turn her into the woman of his dreams.

Instead of being offended that he wanted to change her thus, as he had half expected, Marissa seemed excited, even eager. "It sounds exotic!" she said. "An adventure! I mean, it's safe, isn't it? They won't, like, hold me hostage or anything?"

"Not according to this guy. He said it's all on the up and up. Strictly legal with contracts and the whole bit. But I would want to go out there, of course, and check it out. See if I think it's something that we would be interested in. If you're interested, that is. I certainly don't want to force you into this, Marissa."

"Would you be with me? I wouldn't have to go alone, would I? Is it a real castle? Are there servants?" Marissa was sitting up straight now, looking as eager as a new kitten for a ball of twine. Another delightful game for this little Cinderella.

Tom smiled despite himself, she was impossibly charming. "I really don't even know what it is. It could be a big sham, or a cover up for prostitution or who knows what. But, I'm willing to go take a look, if you're interested."

Marissa looked at Tom through a thick fringe of lashes, consciously coquettish, her mouth a sweet little pout. "I'll do anything for you, Tom. Anything at all." She pressed her arms together, no doubt aware of how it pressed her breasts up and together to create a deep and alluring cleavage. His penis responded, now totally shushing any remaining little warning bells, as he took her in his arms, as firmly ensnared as ever.

Why an electronic book?

We live in the Information Age—an exciting time in the history of human civilization, in which technology rules supreme and continues to progress in leaps and bounds every minute of every day. For a multitude of reasons, more and more avid literary fans are opting to purchase e-books instead of paper books. The question from those not yet initiated into the world of electronic reading is simply: *Why?*

1. *Price.* An electronic title at Ellora's Cave Publishing and Cerridwen Press runs anywhere from 40% to 75% less than the cover price of the exact same title in paperback format. Why? Basic mathematics and cost. It is less expensive to publish an e-book (no paper and printing, no warehousing and shipping) than it is to publish a paperback, so the savings are passed along to the consumer.

2. *Space.* Running out of room in your house for your books? That is one worry you will never have with electronic books. For a low one-time c ost, you can purchase a handheld device specifically designed for e-reading. Many e-readers have large, convenient screens for viewing. Better yet, hundreds of titles can be stored within your new library—on a single microchip. There are a variety of e-readers from different manufacturers. You can also read e-books on your PC or laptop computer. (Please note that Ellora's

Cave does not endorse any specific brands. You can check our websites at www.ellorascave.com or www.cerridwenpress.com for information we make available to new consumers.)

3. *Mobility*. Because your new e-library consists of only a microchip within a small, easily transportable e-reader, your entire cache of books can be taken with you wherever you go.

4. *Personal Viewing Preferences.* Are the words you are currently reading too small? Too large? Too… ANNOYING? Paperback books cannot be modified according to personal preferences, but e-books can.

5. *Instant Gratification.* Is it the middle of the night and all the bookstores near you are closed? Are you tired of waiting days, sometimes weeks, for bookstores to ship the novels you bought? Ellora's Cave Publishing sells instantaneous downloads twenty-four hours a day, seven days a week, every day of the year. Our webstore is never closed. Our e-book delivery system is 100% automated, meaning your order is filled as soon as you pay for it.

Those are a few of the top reasons why electronic books are replacing paperbacks for many avid readers.

As always, Ellora's Cave and Cerridwen Press welcome your questions and comments. We invite you to email us at Comments@ellorascave.com or write to us directly at Ellora's Cave Publishing Inc., 1056 Home Avenue, Akron, OH 44310-3502.

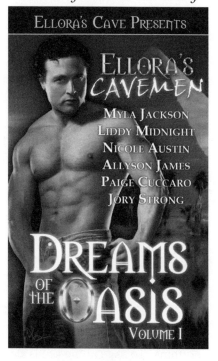

Call Me Barbarian By Liddy Midnight

Princess Cedilla enjoys unprecedented privilege in a society where women are neither seen nor heard. Her life changes when twin barbarian gladiators enter the arena. One glance and Cedilla is irrevocably bound to these Southern warriors — and revealed as half-barbarian herself. Whether in the arena or the bedchamber, Asterix and Apostroph live for the moment — until they find their destined mate. When Cedilla is banished by the Emperor, they devote themselves to satisfying her wildest desires. But the Empire needs Cedilla, and the Empire is intolerant of barbarians...

Dragonmagic By Allyson James

It's hell to be a dragon enslaved. Arys, a powerful silver dragon in human form, is bound to a witch who uses his magic and his body to pleasure her in every way imaginable. When Arys spies Naida, a young woman just coming into her powers, watching Arys performing erotic acts with the witch, he knows that Naida is the key to his freedom. First he must convince Naida she's his true mate and that the power of their sexual play, and her love, will release him.

Fallen For You By Paige Cuccaro

For ten thousand years, Zade's warrior mentality kept him focused on the Watcher's mission — rid the world of the Oscurità fallen angels. And then the witch Isabel came under his care. The Oscurità will be coming to posses her or kill her, drawn by her burgeoning powers. Isabel is a temptation they can't ignore, but neither can Zade. If he succumbs to his feelings, Zade's frozen soul could destroy Isabel. If he resists, his unsatisfied need may cost him everything. To save all he holds dear, Zade must trust that Isabel was born for him, and he has fallen for her.

Spontaneous Combustion By Nicole Austin

Dr. Madailein Flannagan's carnal desires are blazing deep inside, and her best friend Jake Cruise is just the man to fan the flames. But the sexy, bad boy firefighter goes for equally bad girls, and Maddy's afraid she's just not his type. Although lately she has been fantasizing about Jake and a few of his friends... Jake thinks that Maddy is way out of his league, but he knows that she can't refuse a challenge. And he's come up with an irresistible dare guaranteed to send her body up in flames, gain her submission, and maybe even win her heart.

The Ambassador's Widow By Myla Jackson

Chameleon Agent Andre Batello is sent on assignment to "fill in" for an ambassador who died the night before a long-negotiated peace treaty is due to be signed. As part of a special team of individuals with the ability to assume another's identity based on a single strand of DNA, Andre's mission is to infiltrate the ambassador's life and sign that treaty. The one major glitch in his mission: he didn't plan on falling in love with the ambassador's widow.

The Joining By Jory Strong

On the water world of Qumaar, Siria Chaton is a prisoner of her talent. With her credits dwindling, she has few options and little hope for a future. Until Jett and Mozaiic du'Zehren enter her life.

After five years of being a couple, Jett and Mozaiic have gained permission to add a third, a woman, to their joining. They can't believe their good fortune when the woman assigned to them is a water diviner. Now if only she'll accept them as lovers and come home with them to the forbidden desert planet of Adjara.

MAKE EACH DAY MORE EXCITING WITH OUR
ELLORA'S
CAVEMEN
CALENDAR
WWW.ELLORASCAVE.COM

COMING TO A BOOKSTORE NEAR YOU!

ELLORA'S CAVE

Bestselling Authors Tour

UPDATES AVAILABLE AT

WWW.ELLORASCAVE.COM